"Don't tell me you're one of those hopeless romantics who believes love conquers all."

Travis's words came back to Elena. She'd told him she used to believe that...but wasn't sure what she believed anymore. She'd lied. She was still a hopeless romantic.

When she'd married Travis, she'd wanted a marriage built not only on love and desire, but also on mutual respect, and shared hopes and dreams.

In the month before his disappearance, those dreams had flickered out, squashed beneath his sneering derision and casual cruelty. She'd fought with herself every day, wanting out of the marriage, yet still reluctant to give up on her dreams.

Now the "new" Travis was giving her some hope. Maybe he would be the same once he got his memory back. Or maybe fate was somehow giving them a second chance to make those wonderful dreams come true....

Dear Reader,

It's autumn. There's a nip in the air, the light has a special quality it only takes on at this time of year, and soon witches and warlocks (most of them under three feet tall!) will be walking the streets of towns everywhere. And along with them will come vampires, perhaps the most dangerously alluring of all romantic heroes. (The six-foot-tall variety, anyway!) So in honor of the season, this month we're bringing you *Brides of the Night,* a two-in-one collection featuring vampire heroes who are (dare I say it?) to die for. Maggie Shayne continues her wonderful WINGS IN THE NIGHT miniseries with *Twilight Vows,* while Marilyn Tracy lures you in with *Married by Dawn.* Let them wrap you in magic.

We've got more great miniseries going on this month, too. With *Harvard's Education,* Suzanne Brockmann continues her top-selling TALL, DARK AND DANGEROUS miniseries. Readers have been asking for Harvard's story, and now this quintessential tough guy is rewarded with a romance of his own. Then follow our writers out west, as Carla Cassidy begins the saga of MUSTANG, MONTANA, with *Her Counterfeit Husband,* and Margaret Watson returns to CAMERON, UTAH, in *For the Children.* Jill Shalvis, an experienced author making her first appearance here, also knows how great a cowboy hero can be, as she demonstrates in our WAY OUT WEST title, *Hiding Out at the Circle C.* Finally, welcome Hilary Byrnes. This brand-new author is Intimate Moments' WOMAN TO WATCH. And after you read her powerful debut, *Motive, Means...and Marriage?* you *will* be watching—for her next book!

Enjoy! And come back again next month, when we bring you six more of the best and most exciting romance novels around—right here in Silhouette Intimate Moments.

Leslie Wainger

Leslie J. Wainger
Executive Senior Editor

Please address questions and book requests to:
Silhouette Reader Service
U.S.: 3010 Walden Ave., P.O. Box 1325, Buffalo, NY 14269
Canadian: P.O. Box 609, Fort Erie, Ont. L2A 5X3

HER
COUNTERFEIT
HUSBAND

CARLA
CASSIDY

Published by Silhouette Books

America's Publisher of Contemporary Romance

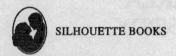

SILHOUETTE BOOKS

ISBN 0-373-07885-4

HER COUNTERFEIT HUSBAND

Copyright © 1998 by Carla Bracale

Printed in U.S.A.

Books by Carla Cassidy

Silhouette Intimate Moments

One of the Good Guys #531
Try To Remember #560
Fugitive Father #604
Behind Closed Doors #778
†*Reluctant Wife* #850
†*Reluctant Dad* #856
‡*Her Counterfeit Husband* #885

Silhouette Romance

Patchwork Family #818
Whatever Alex Wants... #856
Fire and Spice #884
Homespun Hearts #905
Golden Girl #924
Something New #942
Pixie Dust #958
The Littlest Matchmaker #978
The Marriage Scheme #996
Anything for Danny #1048
*Deputy Daddy #1141
*Mom in the Making #1147
*An Impromptu Proposal #1152
*Daddy on the Run #1158
Pregnant with His Child... #1259
*Will You Give My Mommy
  a Baby?* #1315

Silhouette Desire

A Fleeting Moment #784
Under the Boardwalk #882

Silhouette Shadows

Swamp Secrets #4
Heart of the Beast #11
Silent Screams #25
Mystery Child #61

Silhouette Books

Shadows 1993
Devil and the Deep Blue Sea

The Loop
Getting it Right: Jessica

Silhouette Yours Truly

Pop Goes the Question

*The Baker Brood
†Sisters
‡Mustang, Montana

CARLA CASSIDY

had her first Silhouette novel, *Patchwork Family,* published in September of 1991, and since that time she has written over twenty-five novels for various Silhouette lines. She's looking forward to writing many more books and bringing hours of pleasure to her readers.

To Spooky—

who will do anything for a dog bone

Prologue

Elena Richards stood on the cliff, away from the edge, unsure if her rapid heartbeats were from their lovemaking or from her fear of heights.

"That was great, babe."

Suddenly she stiffened as her husband's masculine arms embraced her from behind. For one month she had been Mrs. Travis Richards, and for the last thirty days she'd been desperately trying to tell herself the marriage wasn't a mistake. But she knew deep down in her heart marrying Travis had been the biggest mistake she'd ever made.

She turned around, studying the strong, chiseled lines of his handsome face, seeking some semblance of the man she'd believed him to be. "It wasn't 'great,' Travis. It scared me. You scared me."

"Oh, don't be a baby," he scoffed as he tightened his arms around her. "You know this is my most favorite place. Is it so wrong that I wanted to share it with my favorite girl?''

Part of her anger and fear seeped away beneath the charm of his words. She reached up and touched his mouth, traced the strength of his jaw and tried not to think that only moments ago he had forced her into making love. ''Travis...we need to talk.''

His blue gray eyes flashed impatience. ''I'm not in the mood for one of your serious talks. Can't you just enjoy the moment...the view?'' He threw one arm over her shoulders, then swept his other arm to gesture to the landscape around them.

They stood on a rocky platform, the edge which sloped sharply downward. At the bottom of the gorge the Arganus River swiftly raced.

This was the first time Elena had been up here, although Travis often made the four-hour trip from their ranch to come rock climbing here. He'd insisted she accompany him today, refusing to take no for an answer. Reluctantly she'd agreed, but now all she wanted was to go home.

''Can we go? I'm getting cold,'' she said as she stepped further back from the treacherous edge and buttoned her jacket at her neck.

''You go on to the car. I'll be down in a few minutes.'' He pulled his arm from around her shoulders and stuck his hands in his jeans' pockets. ''I just want to stay here a little while longer.''

Elena hesitated, not wanting to stay but fearful of making her way down the narrow trail to the car alone. A gust of wind blew and she shivered. She knew she'd be warmer in the car and decided to go on ahead. ''I'll see you in a few minutes,'' she said as she headed for the trail back to the car.

She took several steps, then turned back to look at Travis. Her heart quickened at the sight of him, so tall, so handsome. Their courtship had been brief, a whirlwind of passion and promises that after less than a month had culminated in their small wedding at city hall.

She should have dated him longer, she told herself. But he'd been so charming, so persistent. He'd overwhelmed her with his romantic nature, chased away all her doubts beneath his dizzying passion.

Focusing on her slow progress down the path, she avoided looking at the dangerous cliffs and ravines on either side.

It took her nearly twenty minutes to reach the bottom of the trail where they'd parked. She drew a deep gulp of air, able to breath again now that she was off the steep, rocky path.

She dug her keys out of her pocket, got into the car and started the engine, eager for the heater to begin blowing warm air. She wondered if she was cold because of the outside chill or because her heart ached with the knowledge that her marriage to Travis had been a terrible mistake.

He wasn't the man she'd believed him to be. His disregard for her fear up on the cliff and his selfish persistence that they make love had crystallized the knowledge that something had to change.

Within minutes toasty warmth surrounded her. Whether Travis liked it or not, they had to talk, had to discuss where their marriage was headed. She wasn't happy, and she didn't think he was, either. She stared at the mouth of the trail that led upward to the ridge, waiting for Travis to appear.

He never did.

Chapter 1

In those moments between deep slumber and complete awakeness, Elena Richards turned over, her arm automatically seeking the warmth of her husband next to her.

The cold, empty side of the bed forced her to remember. Travis wasn't here. Travis wasn't anywhere. He'd disappeared from that cliff five months ago, as if swallowed by a spaceship.

Pulling the collar of an old shirt closer around her neck, she caught a faint whiff of Travis's cologne. Each morning the minty fragrance grew a little weaker. Soon she would no longer be able to smell his essence on the material.

She sat up, waiting for the wave of morning sickness to strike, surprised as always when it didn't. For the first three months she'd suffered severe morning sickness, but just as the doctor had predicted, the beginning of her fourth month of pregnancy had caused a cessation of the affliction.

She got out of bed, her hand automatically caressing her blossoming belly. The baby. A gift from Travis from the last time she'd seen him...four months and three weeks ago.

On that morning on the cliff, she'd wanted to talk to Travis, to tell him their marriage wasn't working. But she'd never gotten the chance.

Now he was missing. It was the not knowing what happened to him that tormented her, had tormented her every day in the months since his disappearance. Was he alive? Was he dead? Though she didn't know how she felt about him, he was their baby's father.

Shoving aside her thoughts, she showered and dressed quickly, deciding to weed the garden before the heat of the day grew too intense to be outside.

Walking into the kitchen, she was greeted by a welcoming yip from the little black poodle who'd been curled up on the rug in front of the sink. "Good morning, Spooky." She bent down and ruffled the furry pompom head. "You want to go outside?" The poodle danced with pleasure, dark eyes shining like marbles.

Elena smiled and opened the back door. The dog darted outside with the vigor of two-year-old youth, beelining for a bird who instantly flew away from the energetic bundle of black fur.

Elena made coffee, poured herself a cup, then stepped out the back door. The morning smelled of rich earth and fresh dew...the scent of possibilities that always came with the dawn of a new day. For Elena, it only smelled of another day of loneliness, another day of unanswered questions.

She set her coffee mug aside and grabbed a hoe from the small shed. She'd found that if she worked hard enough during the day, exhausted herself with physical activity, then dreams and never-ending questions didn't haunt her sleep.

The ground between the rows of vegetables was hard, and Elena worked the hoe methodically, removing weeds and breaking up the soil. Spooky ran circles around her, then collapsed in the shade beneath the deck, watching Elena with big, adoring eyes.

Elena paused every once in a while, leaning against the hoe to catch her breath and rest her back.

It was during one of these brief respites that she suddenly felt a tingling sensation at the back of her neck. The feeling of being watched.

As the tingle at the nape intensified, Elena looked around the yard. Crazy. With a seven-foot privacy fence enclosing the immediate garden area, it was impossible for anyone to be watching her.

She shook her head, attempting to dismiss her unease and went back to work. In the weeks following Travis's absence, she had put in an enormous garden, finding the work helped get her through each day. The seeds she'd sown now flourished, just as the baby inside her did.

The creak of the gate opening drew her attention. She whirled around to see a tall, dark-haired man enter the yard. She frowned, momentarily half blinded by the morning sun over his shoulder. The shadows from his dark hat combined with the glare of the sun and obscured his features.

Spooky barked and approached the man cautiously. A quick sniff and the dog returned to the shadows beneath the deck.

A cloud skittered in front of the sun, effectively blocking the harsh glare and the man's features came into view. Elena gasped and dropped the hoe.

"Travis." His name spilled from her lips, a sigh of disbelief, a breath of stunned shock. She took several steps toward him, then stopped, unsure if she'd lost her mind and had simply conjured up a chimera to replace what had been lost.

"Elena?"

His voice, so achingly familiar, broke her inertia. With a sob, she launched herself toward him, throwing her arms around his neck, and buried her face in the fresh-smelling front of his cotton shirt. There was a moment he remained stiff, unyielding, then his arms went around her.

A million questions and a million different emotions whirled around inside her. Tears fell onto his chest as sobs choked her. For the moment she didn't care that she'd known he wasn't the kind of man she wanted to spend her life with. He was alive. The baby's father was alive.

As she held him close, she noticed subtle differences. Thinner. He was definitely thinner than before. He smelled different, too. Rather than the minty scent of his favorite cologne, he smelled of an earthy spice fragrance she found both mysterious and appealing.

Her initial shock began to fade, transforming relief and joy into confusion and anger. She'd been in limbo for almost five months, not knowing if he was alive or dead. She balled her hands into fists and hit him in the chest. "Where have you been? I've been so scared, so worried. What happened?"

He tensed and stepped away from her assault. For a

moment they stared at each other, Elena drinking in his presence, still unable to believe he was here.

His hair was shorter, more neatly styled than it had been the last time she'd seen him. Although his face was thinner, it contained the same features that had haunted her night after night. Blue gray eyes ringed with dark lush lashes, a straight nose, full lips and a slight cleft in the square chin.

She scanned his face, then directed her gaze back to his eyes...eyes that appeared subdued, with a hint of bewilderment. "Travis? Let's go inside where we can talk."

He nodded and as she led him toward the house the sun once again disappeared behind a cloud, casting a shadow of darkness to the earth. An inexplicable shiver worked its way up Elena's spine. Her husband was back, a husband she hadn't been sure she wanted. At least now there would be some closure...no more nights of wondering what had happened.

Spooky followed them inside, short tail wagging. "Coffee?" Elena asked as they entered the house. How ludicrous, she thought. My husband has just returned after an unexplained agonizingly long absence, and I'm calmly offering him coffee.

Equally as ridiculous, he nodded his head and sank into a chair at the table, as if it had only been the space of a single morning since he'd last sat there.

Spooky settled beneath his chair. Elena tried to rationalize the dog's odd actions. During Elena and Travis's courtship and marriage, Spooky had never taken to Travis. In the first weeks when they'd been dating, Spooky had growled and shown displeasure with him. In the weeks following the wedding, the dog had settled for keeping distant, usually eyeing him balefully from across the room. Suddenly he was cuddling up next to him, as if he were his master. Maybe Spooky had missed Travis in his absence as well.

Elena poured him a cup of coffee, then sat across from Travis, confused, bewildered and still more than a little angry.

For a long moment neither said a word. Elena cupped her hands around her coffee mug, the warmth reassuring. She felt as if reality had vanished and somehow she'd fallen into a dream.

"Travis?" She reached out and touched his hand, needing to know what had happened, where he'd been for the last four and a half months. He pulled away from her touch and swiped a hand through his hair. "For God sakes, talk to me."

His eyes met hers, haunted. "You're pregnant," he blurted.

Elena's hand went automatically to her stomach. If he asked if the child were his, he would destroy her. She didn't give him an opportunity to ask. "That day up on the mountain ridge, the last time we were together, we conceived a child." She rubbed her hand over her stomach lovingly. "Don't you remember?"

Again he raked a hand through his thick hair. "No. I don't."

"But you must. It was our one-month anniversary and you made me…I mean, we drove to the mountain and we…we made love." She tried not to focus on the unpleasantness of that memory. "It was the day you disappeared. I waited for you in the car, but you never came back."

"I don't remember the ridge." He paused, then added softly. "And what's worse, I don't remember you."

His words hung in the air. Elena's breath caught in her chest, as if somehow his startling confessions had displaced all the oxygen from the room.

"I...I don't understand," she finally gasped.

He frowned, a deep wrinkle cutting through his broad forehead as he stared down into his coffee mug. "Several months ago I was pulled from the Arganus River by an old backwoodsman. According to him, I was more dead than alive. He fed me, nursed me and fixed a couple broken bones. When I regained consciousness, I realized I didn't know who I was or how I'd come to be in the river."

"And now?" she asked breathlessly.

He shrugged and looked at her once again, his eyes dark and pained. "Over the last couple of weeks, names came back to me. My name. Your name. And the backwoodsman drove me here. But there are no memories...nothing." The darkness of his eyes dissipated somewhat. "I'm sorry...I just can't remember."

Sympathy ripped through her at his words, as did the release of any anger. How could she be angry with him? He'd been hurt so badly, he'd developed some sort of amnesia.

"Tell me about the ridge," he said. "You said we were on the mountain ridge the last time you saw me?"

She nodded. "It's part of the Bitterroot Range. It's a four-hour drive from here. You used to go climbing there. You'd been after me since the moment we met to go with you. That...that day was the first time I went."

He leaned forward, his gaze so intense it was as if

he were peering into her soul. "Tell me what happened up there. Tell me everything, from the minute we arrived."

Elena drew a deep breath, trying to get past the emotion, beyond the trauma that thoughts of that day always brought. She stood and left the table, unable to look at him and calmly recite the events of that day.

"You awakened me in the middle of the night and insisted that we go to the ridge. You wanted to be there in time to see the sunrise." As she spoke, she paced back and forth across the kitchen floor. The warped uneven linoleum crackled beneath her footsteps. She didn't want to think about his taunts, the derision he'd used to get her to agree to go with him.

"You had a flashlight and together we went to the top. We got there just as the sun began to peek over the horizon." She leaned against the refrigerator, remembering that morning when dawn had streaked the morning clouds with pinks and lavenders and the sun had been an orange ball amid the exquisite sky colors. The mountains had been a lush purple, their peaks whitened with winter snows. Despite her fear, she'd been awed by the beauty and glad he'd talked her into coming.

She averted her gaze from him before continuing, unable to sustain eye contact with this man who looked like her husband, but who gazed at her as if she were a stranger. "After the sunrise, you...we...made love."

Frowning, she rubbed her forehead, not wanting to remember how he'd forced her, how he'd laughingly rolled her closer and closer to the edge of the ridge.

She felt his gaze on her and looked up to see him staring at her. "What?" he asked. "Is there something you aren't telling me?"

"No...that's it." A flush warmed her face. Why tell him she'd almost hated him while he'd physically possessed her? Why tell him that it had been at that moment that she'd realized she couldn't stay married to him? "Shouldn't you go to a doctor? See about this amnesia?" she asked.

"I've been. The doctor believes time will eventually rectify the problem. He suggested I surround myself with familiar things, familiar people. That's why I came here."

He looked around the room. Elena followed his gaze, knowing he was taking in the old flooring, the wood cabinets that no longer closed properly and the stained, chipped porcelain sink.

"We were going to fix up the place," she said softly, feeling the need to defend the ranch house she'd bought for a song because it needed so much work. She'd had so many plans. They were going to buy cattle, get a couple of horses and transform the old deserted ranch into a working one. Plans and dreams she'd believed Travis had shared until their brief marriage had told her otherwise.

Those plans and dreams had slowly died beneath Travis's coldness, his thoughtlessness, his utter disregard for her during their brief marriage.

He nodded and took a sip of his coffee. "So, what happened after we made love?"

Elena sat back down at the table. "I got cold. I went back to the car and you said you'd follow in just a few minutes." Knots of stress pressed heavily against her chest. "But you never came back to the car."

"How long was it before you came looking for me?"

Guilt suffused her. A guilt she'd suffered every night

for the past four and a half months. "A long time. I fell asleep." The confession tore from her and she gulped air to stop the tears that burned at her eyes. She stared down at the table, unable to look at him as the full brunt of her guilt swept through her. "The car was warm, and you'd awakened me so early. I dozed off and woke up two hours later. When I realized you were still gone, I was frantic."

"Then what happened?" His voice was soft, softer than she could ever remember hearing it before. "Did you go looking for me?"

She flinched, guilt deepening. "I did the best I could," she said breathlessly. "I couldn't go back up that trail alone. I...I'm frightened of heights. The only way I got up there before was with you holding on to me, helping me."

She swallowed, the metallic taste of remembered fear in her mouth. She'd stood at the base of the narrow, steep trail and fought with herself, torn between the need to get up there to find him and the utter panic that kept her rooted in place. "I yelled and yelled your name and when there was no answer, I drove to the park ranger station."

"And they launched a search for me?"

"A massive manhunt. And for the next week they dragged the river every day."

"So they believed I fell over the edge into the river below?"

She nodded.

He swiped a hand down his face and looked at her. "I'm tired, and I'm not up to one hundred percent yet."

For the first time Elena noticed the lines of weariness that radiated from the corners of his eyes, noticed the travel-wrinkled condition of his clothing and the heavy growth of whiskers along his jawline. He looked beyond exhaustion, steeped in confusion, and she realized this was just as difficult for him as it was for her.

She was glad he was alive, still had some residual feelings for him, but there was no way she would go back into a marriage that hadn't been working in the first place. Still, she couldn't very well throw him out. He had no idea who he was; he had no other place to go. And he hadn't known that she intended to ask him for a divorce on that fateful day.

"Of course, you'll want to clean up. I'll show you to our room."

He stood, and she led him down the hallway toward the master bedroom, oddly embarrassed that she hadn't yet made the bed and that her clothing from the night before was draped over the chair in the corner.

"I'm sorry...I wasn't expecting you." She grabbed the clothes off the chair and balled them into a bundle in her arms. She looked at where he stood, his broad shoulders nearly filling the doorway.

"I don't think..." His voice trailed off. He drew a deep breath and tried again. "I'm not ready for this." He kept his gaze averted from hers. "Is there a spare room where I can stay? You know, until we're more comfortable with each other?"

Elena breathed a sigh of relief. Yes, it would be easier to deal with all this if they were in separate rooms. "Of course. You can stay in the guest room."

She led him into the smaller bedroom and watched as he walked around the room, touching the furniture, eyeing the pictures on the wall as if seeking some sliver of memory to cling to.

"All your clothes are in the closet in our bedroom, and the bathroom is just across the hall," she said, wondering if things could get any more awkward.

"Thank you." He sank down on the bed.

Elena left the room and went back in the kitchen.

She scooped up Spooky in her arms and sank down at the table. Stroking the dog's furry neck, she tried to sort through her emotions. "He's back, Spooky," she whispered softly.

Travis was back, and suddenly her life was more complicated than ever before. She had loved him once, but that had been before he'd shown her his negative traits. His anger and bullying, his selfishness and cold heart.

In truth, she had fallen in love with the facade he'd presented to her before the marriage...the facade of a man who didn't really exist. But now that she knew what kind of man Travis really was, she couldn't go back to that.

She stroked Spooky once again, then touched her tummy, where the stir of life fluttered for a moment. Regret weighed down her heart. Her regrets weren't because she was pregnant. No, she couldn't regret the miracle of life inside of her. But she'd never dreamed she would be a single parent, raising a child on her own. But that's exactly what she intended to do.

She would allow Travis to remain here to heal. But when he got his memories back, she would tell him she wanted a divorce.

Chapter 2

He'd never been fond of lying and had always tried to do it as little as possible. The lies he'd told to Elena left a bitter taste in his mouth.

Contrary to what he'd told her, he hadn't gotten a ride to Mustang, Montana, from a backwoodsman who found him in the river. It had taken him a day of straight driving to get here from his apartment in California.

His car was now parked on the other side of town in a grocery store parking lot—where hopefully it wouldn't draw any unwarranted attention for the duration of his stay. He didn't intend to be in town long. He'd gotten a ride from the store to the ranch with a taciturn farmer who'd allowed him to sit in the back of his pickup.

He adjusted the water temperature in the shower, then shucked off the travel-weary clothes and stepped beneath the warm spray.

He sighed in pleasure as the water pummeled him, pleased by the water pressure belied by the antiquated plumbing.

As the water eased taut muscles, he grabbed the bar of soap and began to lather. It had been at his last stop, at a small gas station outside of town, where his plan had finally become clear in his head. The attendant, a young man with big ears and apparently an equally big mouth for listening and repeating gossip, had eyed him in stunned surprise.

"Aren't you Travis Richards?" he'd asked. "Everyone thought you were dead."

In that instant Trent had realized how easy it would be to step into his brother's shoes, walk right into his life and try to find out exactly what had happened to his twin brother.

He thought about his brother's wife. Elena. Her name conjured up visions of a dark, exotic woman with a lush figure and passion red lips. The vision wasn't so far removed from reality.

Her hair had been a mass of dark silk, caught at her nape in a green ribbon that perfectly matched her eyes. Her high cheekbones and the slight almond shape to her eyes gave her face an exotic flavor. Her lips, although not overly red, were full and ripe.

He'd opened the garden gate just an inch and had watched her for long minutes before finally stepping into the garden. From the back, as she'd worked, he'd had no hint of her condition. Shock had riveted through him when she'd turned to face him, displaying her pregnant stomach.

Forcing thoughts of Elena from his mind, he bent his head beneath the nozzle spray.

The past couple of months had been difficult, both physically and emotionally. Not only had he been up to his ears in the usual work at his detective agency, but he was also dealing with the heartache of helplessly watching his mother die.

He'd received a letter a little over six months ago from Travis, bragging that he'd met a fine-looking filly named Elena and they'd gotten married. The letter had been filled with Travis's usual grandiose dreams...he was well on his way to huge wealth and a life of leisure. Enclosed with the letter had been a life insurance policy for half a million dollars, the beneficiary Elena Richards.

Trent ducked his head beneath the nozzle once again, knowing what he needed more than anything was sleep. Everything was muddied in his head. Maybe after a couple hours of rest, things would be less confusing, more clear. He'd only recently known that Travis was missing. His secretary had been going through missing persons reports and had brought Trent the one detailing his brother's disappearance.

"Look, boss...this guy could be your twin," she'd exclaimed. "He looks like you and he even has your last name." She'd eyed him curiously.

Trent had taken the report and stared at the picture. "He *is* my twin," he'd replied.

Stepping out of the shower, Trent grabbed a towel and dried off, his thoughts once again returning to Elena. He hadn't a clue what to expect.

That she was beautiful hadn't been a surprise. He'd expected nothing less. His brother had always had great taste in women. The soft vulnerability that had darkened her eyes to a bottle green had been a surprise, as had the swell of her pregnancy.

He pulled on one of the shirts he'd found in the master bedroom closet, uncomfortable with the muscle-cut sleeves and V-neck style. The jeans were a little loose in the waist, but the length was perfect. Still, he felt as if he were stepping into another man's life.

And that's exactly what he was doing.

He placed the towel and dirty clothes in the hamper, then left the bathroom and went across the hall to the guest room. He stretched out on the bed, pleased to find the mattress firm rather than soft and too giving. Exhaustion from his travel and the turmoil of the last several months tugged at him. He stared at the ceiling, where the midmorning sun cast intricate patterns as it drifted through the white lacy curtains.

For long moments sleep remained elusive as his mind whirled. He needed to find out what had happened on the ridge, if Travis had really fallen, or perhaps foul play was involved. Trent was sure Travis had created a handful of enemies knowing how crazy his twin could be.

Or was it possible Elena and Travis were working together to scam the insurance company? A half a million dollars was a lot of money. Certainly it would go a long way in fixing up this dump Elena called home.

Elena didn't look like a criminal, but Trent had worked enough cases as a P.I. to know beautiful women and handsome men could be as crooked as anyone. Still, she'd said nothing to indicate any kind of culpability. But why would she if she believed he had amnesia?

One thing was clear. In order to uncover the truth, he had to get close to Elena, discover exactly what kind of a woman she was. The only way to find out what had been happening in Travis's life was to become Travis.

He closed his eyes, deciding at least for the moment to give in to the sweet oblivion of sleep.

He slept long and hard, dreamless sleep that assuaged his exhaustion but untangled none of his internal conflict. When he opened his eyes, he realized he must have slept away the day.

The golden glow of dusk filtered through the window, and although the room was stifling with the residual heat of the day, a gentle evening breeze stirred the curtains.

He thought of his attractive apartment, where the air-conditioning would be humming and a six pack of cold beer awaited him in the refrigerator. He wished he were there now, with nothing more pressing on his mind than the everyday hassles of his business.

He got out of bed, washed his face in the bathroom, then went down the hallway toward the kitchen where the scent of cooking and the clatter of silverware foretold of Elena's presence.

He paused in the doorway, instantly seeing her. She hummed beneath her breath, a sweet, winsome tune he didn't recognize, while she checked on something in the oven. The poodle stood and stretched from the braided rug near the back door. She approached him with tail wagging, toenails clicking against the floor.

"Hey, girl," he said, bending down to scratch her head.

Elena whirled around in surprise. "Oh, you're awake," she proclaimed. "Good, supper is ready." She smiled at him, a sweet, shy smile that was at odds with his suspicions of her. "I made your favorite. Swiss steak."

He forced a smile. He hated Swiss steak. "Great," he replied, attempting to interject enthusiasm into his tone. Spooky nudged his hand, looking for another caress.

"I guess it really is true that absence makes the heart grow fonder," Elena said, her voice colored with a touch of bewilderment. "Spooky didn't want anything to do with you before."

She turned back to the oven and pulled out a large baking dish. "Why don't you sit down, it will just take a minute to get the food on the table."

"Can I help?" he offered.

She looked at him, again with an expression of bewilderment. "Let me guess," he said dryly. "I never offered to help with the meals before."

"I...no...you didn't." She appeared flustered. "Please, have a seat. It will just take me a minute."

Trent sat down, trying to imagine his brother in this domestic setting. It was impossible. Travis had been as domesticated as the wild horses that had once roamed this area.

As Elena bustled to get the meal on the table, Trent watched her and found it hard to believe that this dark-haired slip of a woman might have managed to do what nobody else had...tame Travis.

Was it possible Travis had really fallen in love, married Elena and had intended to make a life here for himself? He frowned. It was like wondering if a coyote could suddenly become a vegetarian.

"We'll need to talk to Sheriff Wilder," Elena said as she joined him at the table.

Trent looked at her curiously.

"He'll want to know that…you're alive."

Trent nodded hesitantly. He hadn't considered the authorities, the fact that he was perpetrating a fraud by pretending to be his brother. But he didn't know what else to do.

"First thing tomorrow morning, I'd like you to take me back up to the ridge where…uh…I fell," he said.

"Why?"

Her eyes flared wide, and for just a moment he saw sheer terror in their depths. He remembered her telling him of her fear of heights. "You won't have to go to the ridge…you can wait in the car or something."

She recovered quickly and passed him the platter of steak. "Travis, it's dangerous up there. You slipped once and almost died. Why…why would you want to go up there again?"

"It might jog my memory." He speared a piece of the steak with a fork and placed it on his plate, then set the platter down. "You want me to get my memory back, don't you Elena?" he asked softly.

Her gaze didn't meet his. "Of course," she replied.

Their dinner conversation was stilted and sparse. Trying to find a topic of conversation with a man who suffered amnesia was difficult indeed. She talked about the weather, chattered inanely about national politics and the latest newspaper headlines. Anything…anything to fill the awkward silences that prevailed whenever she stopped talking.

After dinner, he surprised her by helping clean off the table, then grabbed a dish towel to dry as she washed the dishes. He apparently once again registered her surprise.

They worked in silence for a few minutes. "So, before I fell, what did I used to do while you did the dishes?" he asked, finally breaking the uncomfortable quiet.

She shrugged and handed him a glass to dry. "Sometimes you'd watch television. Most of the time you went into town and had a few beers with friends at the Roundup."

"The Roundup?"

She nodded. It had been a bone of contention between them. She hadn't understood why he'd felt the need to run off practically every night instead of spending cozy evenings with her. "It's a bar in town...kind of wild. Not the place where you would take your wife." She frowned, hearing a whisper of anger in her words.

"And you didn't have a problem with that?"

Using a soapy sponge, she washed off the last plate, remembering her disappointment the first time Travis had disappeared after an evening meal. "You warned me before we got married that you needed a lot of personal space."

She handed him the plate, the anger surging and sweeping through her as she remembered those evenings when, as a newlywed, she'd been left alone while he'd been out enjoying "personal space."

"You're angry," he observed as he took the plate from her.

A flush warmed her face as she drained the dishwater and reached for a towel to dry her hands. "No," she protested. "Well, perhaps. I'd forgotten until now how much it bothered me when you'd go off alone in the evenings.''

"Did you tell me you didn't like it?"

She placed the towel by the sink and turned to face him. "Not really. At first I didn't want to make waves. And when I did finally mention it, you told me to stop being a baby, that you were married, not in prison.'' Pain shot through her at the memory of his harsh words.

He reached out and touched her cheek softly with the pad of his index finger. The touch stirred a nearly forgotten warmth inside her. He withdrew his hand and stepped back from her.

"Was I always a bastard?" he asked.

A nervous giggle escaped her lips at the unexpectedness of his question. "Yes...no..." Her laughter died as confusion swept through her. Perhaps now was the time to tell him that she wanted a divorce, that the marriage had been a horrible mistake. Still, his eyes held a strange vulnerability that made it impossible for her to tell him now. "You could also be quite charming," she finally said.

He nodded, a muscle knotting at his jaw. "I noticed a couple of chairs on the front porch," he said. "Why don't we go sit...talk for a little while?"

Elena nodded, knowing if he remembered nothing about himself, there were questions he'd want answered. Spooky followed them outside. The evening air was warm.

Travis sank into one of the wooden chairs, then laughed as Spooky jumped up in his lap. His laughter sounded different than that of Elena's memory. More full-bodied, deeper, it rolled over her, through her with warmth.

"I can't believe how she's suddenly so taken with you," Elena said as she watched Spooky turn over on her back, bearing her belly for Travis to scratch.

He smiled down at the black poodle. "I guess she's had a change of heart." He leaned back in his chair and looked around.

Elena followed his gaze, her heart swelling as she took in the landscape before them. Lush grass carpeted the open range that seemed to stretch to forever.

"Did we buy this place together, or did you live here before you met me?" he asked.

"I bought it eight months before we met. My parents died in a plane accident and I got an initial settlement from the insurance company. I used that money to settle here."

She looked at him. "We had big plans for this place. We intended to turn it into a prosperous ranch."

He frowned, his gaze once again surveying the property. "Looks like it's going to take a lot of hard work and money to accomplish that."

She looked at the corral and nearby barn. The shed listed precariously in one direction, and the barn's paint was peeling and faded. The corral timbers were rotten, most had fallen to the ground rather than providing any sort of enclosure. "At the time we made those plans, money wasn't an issue."

He raised a dark eyebrow and gazed at her quizzically. "Why, are you independently wealthy?"

"I was." She sighed and linked her fingers together over her burgeoning tummy. "When my parents died, they not only left me an insurance settlement, but also a rather large trust fund. I could receive it for two more years, until I turn twenty-seven, but I was receiving the interest on it each month.''

''Was? What happened?''

Once again Elena focused her gaze away from him. ''A month before you disappeared, the money was stolen.''

He muttered a curse beneath his breath, startling Spooky who jumped off his lap and instead curled up beneath his chair. ''How much money are we talking about?''

Elena drew a deep breath. ''Almost three quarters of a million dollars. You told me it didn't matter,'' she hurriedly added, ''that we'd still make the ranch work and grow.''

Oh, how she remembered that day, when a representative from the accounting firm had shown up here to tell her the bad news. For her, the money had never really been important other than as a means to her dreams. And her dreams had been in this land...and in Travis.

''At first, when they told us the money was gone, you went wild,'' she continued. ''You were livid, threatened to sue everyone who'd ever had anything to do with the accounting firm. Then, once you settled down, you told me we'd still make things work out here, that it would just take longer, be a little harder.''

''Did I have a job? What did I do?'' he asked. He sat forward, the movement bringing to her his scent. So evocative...so male. She drew a deep breath, noting again that he no longer smelled of the cologne he'd worn before.

''When we first met, you told me you'd come to Mustang to find work, that you'd been down in Texas working a ranch for the last couple of years, but the owner had sold out and you were left jobless.''

He nodded slowly, as if digesting the information. ''How did we meet?''

Elena smiled, the memory of that day washing over her with pleasure. ''I'd gone into town to buy some supplies and ended up getting coffee at Debbie's Diner, a hole-in-the-wall on Main Street. I was sitting in a booth alone, reading the paper when you came in.'' Her breath quickened at the memory and a flush warmed her cheeks. ''You were the most handsome, sexy cowboy I'd ever seen.'' Her cheeks grew hotter. ''You swept me off my feet. Within four weeks we were married.''

''Pretty fast courtship,'' he observed and she was surprised to hear a bit of disapproval in his tone.

''Yes, it was,'' she agreed. ''But at the time, the brevity of it all didn't matter. It just felt right.''

He leaned back and swiped a hand through his hair. The gesture spoke of hopelessness and Elena felt its echo in her heart. ''None of it rings any bells? Seems the least bit familiar?'' she asked.

He shook his head. ''It's like you're talking about somebody else. It's a nice story but doesn't have anything to do with me.''

The echo of hopelessness rang louder in Elena's heart. She wanted him to remember, needed to get him out before she fell victim to his charm once again.

Their conversation was interrupted by the appearance of a truck, the wheels stirring a cloud of dust as it approached. ''That's Cameron,'' Elena said.

''Cameron?''

''My brother.'' She stood as the truck pulled to a halt in front of the house. She wondered if he'd come to deliver news about Lydia Walsh, the trustee who had absconded with their trust funds.

She smiled as he got out of the truck, a long, lean drink of water in dusty jeans and a T-shirt. Her smile faded as he didn't return it. She tensed as he got closer and she saw the fire of anger that lit his eyes. "Cam…" she protested as he swept past her and stood before Travis.

"So, it's true. The prodigal husband has returned."

Travis set Spooky on the porch, then stood, as if to meet the unspoken challenge in Cameron's eyes. Before he could reply, Elena placed a restraining hand on Cameron's arm. "Cam…please. He has amnesia. He doesn't remember anything."

Cameron looked at Travis dubiously. "Amnesia?"

Travis nodded. "How did you know I was here?"

Cameron took a step backward, his hands unclenching at his sides. "Mustang is a small town. Gossip spreads quickly. So, if you have amnesia, how did you know to come here?" Cameron's eyes narrowed in suspicion.

"I remember some things. This place. Elena."

"Cam, he's not a criminal," Elena protested.

"As far as I'm concerned, a man who leaves his wife pregnant and alone for over four months is as close to a criminal as it gets," Cameron returned.

"He didn't know I was pregnant, and he came back as soon as he remembered." Elena squeezed her brother's arm, knowing his anger was a result of his love for her and his need to protect her from any further heartache, but she wanted him to back off. "Do you have any news about Lydia Walsh?" she asked in an effort to direct his attention from Travis.

"No, nothing." He sighed in frustration. "But I'm not giving up. Between law enforcement and me, we'll get her." His dark eyes played on Elena. "You all right?" She knew he was talking about Travis's sudden reappearance.

"I'm fine," she assured him. "You want something to drink?" She glanced back at Travis, who remained standing as if unsure what to expect.

"No. I just wanted to come by and see if what I heard was true. I've got to get back home." Cameron walked off the porch and Elena went with him, leaving Travis, who sank back into the chair.

Cameron opened his truck door, but paused before sliding in behind the wheel. "Are you sure you're okay?" He cast a dark glance back at Travis. "This doesn't feel right to me...him just reappearing after so long."

"Cam, please. This is something I have to sort out on my own. Travis and I have a lot of things to talk about, but it's going to take some time. He needs to get his memory back."

Again a scowl crossed Cameron's handsome face. "I just don't want to see you hurt anymore."

Elena smiled at her older brother and placed a palm against his strong jaw. "I promise I'll be fine, Cam."

He got into the truck. "Call me if you need anything, otherwise I'll be in touch when I have any news on Lydia."

Elena watched as he took off, the back of the truck fishtailing slightly as he pulled away. She watched until his truck disappeared, then turned back and joined Travis on the porch.

"Is it just since my disappearance, or has your brother always hated me?" Travis asked.

Elena eased into the chair next to him with a small laugh. "Don't take it to heart. Cameron pretty much hates everyone."

"He looked like he was ready to take off my head." Travis gazed at her for a long moment. "'Course I can't say as I blame him. I'd want to tear apart a man who left my sister pregnant and all alone without any explanation."

Elena shrugged. "You didn't intend to fall off the cliff or get amnesia."

"Speaking of the cliff…how about taking a ride there tomorrow morning?"

Elena hesitated. God help her, but she didn't want to go back there. That last day with Travis had been a nightmare, his disappearance lengthening the nightmare into months.

Still, she knew it might be exactly the catalyst that would cause him to regain his memory. "Okay. We'll leave right after breakfast. It's a long drive to make there and back in one day." She stood. "I think I'm going to call it a day and go to bed," she said. She walked to the door, but hesitated and looked back at him as he called her name.

"I know the last couple of months must have been hell for you," he said. "I just want you to know that I'm sorry."

Her breath caught in her chest as his words seemed to wrap around her heart. She nodded. "You'll lock up when you come in?"

"Yes."

She left him there, in the purple glow of deepening

night shadows. A man with no memories except the ones she gave him.

Elena went into her bedroom and changed into the old shirt that served as a nightgown. Turning out the light then sliding beneath the sheets, she thought of the man she had left on the porch. She rolled over on her back and stared at the ceiling where the rising moon splayed fingers of light as it seeped through the opened blinds.

She hoped he got his memory back in the morning when they got to the mountain ridge. The sooner she could tell him she wanted a divorce, the better.

The man who had walked into her yard this afternoon looked like her husband, but Travis didn't speak with soft tones, didn't help with the evening dishes, and certainly wouldn't allow the words *I'm sorry* to cross his lips.

This man, her husband...this stranger, was a threat because he appeared to be the embodiment of the fantasy man she'd once believed Travis to be...a fantasy she'd quickly realized didn't exist.

He had to get his memory back quickly...because she absolutely refused to make the same mistake again. No matter how sweet his words, no matter how many dishes he washed...she refused to fall in love with him again.

Chapter 3

"The authorities found this on a small ledge the morning that you disappeared," Elena said the next morning as she set a backpack on the table before Trent. "It was yours."

He pulled the bright red pack toward him. "Where was it found?"

"It was caught on some roots partway down the side of the cliff. Your driver's license is in one of the pockets."

Trent opened the fastener and pulled out a water bottle and a rolled-up jacket. In the side zipper he found the license. He pulled it out and tucked it away in his jeans' pocket, then looked back at Elena, unsure what to say.

It had been that way from the moment they'd met that morning in the kitchen. As they'd sat at the table and drank coffee, the conversation had been stilted and awkward.

"Maybe we should be on our way," he finally said.

She nodded and placed their empty cups in the sink.

Within minutes they were headed out in her car. Trent was behind the wheel as they drove away from the little town of Mustang and toward the Bitterroot Range in the distance.

The rising sun and blue skies chased away the last of the night clouds, promising a clear day. As they traveled, they passed ranches, big spreads and smaller ones, each with a corral full of horses and cattle grazing on pastures of green grass.

Trent barely noticed the scenery. His head spun with the bits and pieces of information he'd gleaned so far, puzzle pieces that didn't quite fit together to make an entire picture.

The backpack had surprised him. She'd told him it had been found hanging off roots halfway down the ridge…evidence of a fall. And yet, Trent didn't feel his brother's death. No emptiness resounded in any place in his heart. He'd always assumed if something happened to Travis, he'd know…no matter how many miles separated them. He'd know with a twin's peculiar extrasensory perception.

"Are you comfortable enough?" he asked, directing one of the car air vents toward her. Although early, already the sun was bright, indicating another unusually warm day.

"I'm fine." She offered him a hesitant smile.

Trent gripped the steering wheel more tightly. She was so different than what he'd expected of his brother's wife. Softer…more vulnerable, she exuded an emotional frailty that surprised him.

In their teenage years, Travis had always been drawn to the "bad girls," the ones whose eyes radiated knowledge of sin. The only time he'd gone after the more innocent women was in order to hurt somebody. Usually in order to hurt Trent.

He drew a deep breath, realizing he clenched the steering wheel so hard his knuckles were white and his hands threatened to cramp. He consciously forced himself to relax and shoved away thoughts of those distant days. His brother's sins had been his heartaches, but that had been in the past.

He struggled to find a safe topic to breach the silence that had grown between them. "Is your brother married?" he asked, remembering the handsome, intense young man who'd looked as if he was ready to throttle somebody.

"No. Cameron keeps himself pretty isolated from people." She hesitated a moment, then continued, "He had a bad experience with a woman several years ago. She was killed. I don't think he's ever recovered. He's afraid to trust in love again."

"What does he do for a living?" Trent found the last of his tension leaving him with the conversation topic being safe and distant.

"He was a bounty hunter. Officially, he quit about six months ago. He bought an old place about ten miles south of ours and intended to ranch, but then our trust funds disappeared and a month later you did as well. For the last couple of months he's been searching for you and for Lydia Walsh."

"Lydia Walsh?"

"The trustee who disappeared with our trust funds."

"How exactly did that happen? Aren't trust funds usually administered by banks?" Trent focused on the road, trying to ignore how attractive she looked as the sun streaked in the window and played in her dark hair.

She hadn't braided it that morning. It flowed loose and long down her back, a rich, thick curtain of shiny strands. It was far too easy to imagine the fresh clean scent of it, the feel of it as it flowed through his fingertips.

She sighed and in his peripheral vision he saw her fold her hands primly in her lap. "Yes, generally they are handled by banks, but my parents didn't trust banks. Lydia Walsh is the daughter of good friends of my parents. She owned an accounting firm and my parents trusted her to handle the trust funds. A little over five months ago Lydia disappeared from the company and her home. When the smoke cleared, Cameron's and my trust fund money was gone."

"Was his trust fund as big as yours?"

She nodded. "My parents lived a frugal life, but my father had a real talent for investments. At the time of their death, my brother and I were shocked to learn just how successful he had been."

"It must have been even more of a shock to have that kind of money in the bank and suddenly have it disappear," he observed. He felt her gaze on him and turned to her.

In the depths of her green eyes he thought he saw a glimmer of accusation. "The money was never very important to me. Granted, it would have been nice to eventually have it to invest in the ranch, but having never had it, it's difficult to miss it."

"But yesterday you mentioned the missing money bothered me."

Her gaze shifted from him. Instead she stared out the window as she twisted the plain gold wedding band around her finger. "Yes, at least for the first couple of days after we found out it was gone. Like I told you last night, you threatened to sue anyone and everyone, but then you calmed down."

She turned and looked at him again, the green of her eyes clear and unfettered with emotion. "You told me we'd build our own fortune, that you'd married me not knowing that I would be wealthy so nothing had really changed."

Trent frowned. Something didn't ring true. He knew his brother well enough to know Travis wouldn't have so easily gotten over a stolen fortune that was within his reach.

Travis loved money, and he'd spent his life trying to gain as much cash as possible with as little work as possible. No, he wouldn't have been easily pacified with the loss of a fortune. Unless Travis had truly fallen in love with this woman. For some reason this thought unsettled Trent.

"Shall we stop for some breakfast?" he asked as he spotted a sign advertising a truck stop ahead.

"Sounds good to me," she agreed.

Minutes later as Trent slid in across from Elena at a booth in the truck stop, he was again impressed by this woman his brother had married.

She was beautiful, but it was a quiet beauty. She wore no makeup that he could discern, but her lashes were thick and dark and her skin lightly tanned and unblemished.

In the past, Travis had always liked flamboyant women, ones who dressed colorfully and didn't know the fine art of subtle makeup. Elena's dress was a light gray, tight enough to display the attractive curve of her breasts, but loose enough to hide the small swell of her stomach.

"You're staring at me," she said, her cheeks stained with the color of a blush.

"Sorry." Trent grabbed the menu and opened it, unsure what it was about her that somehow unsettled him.

"It's all right," she replied, although when he looked at her again he noted the color of her cheeks had intensified. "I'm sure this all must be frightening for you."

"Frightening?"

She nodded. "I mean, I can't imagine not remembering anything about myself or my life. It must be horrible to know I'm your wife and yet not remember anything about me or our life together."

A surge of guilt welled up inside Trent. He should tell her. He should tell her the truth that he wasn't her husband, but rather Travis's twin brother. And yet he was reluctant to lose the one little edge he had in finding out exactly what had been going on in his brother's life before his disappearance.

Just a little while longer, he promised himself, then he would tell her the truth. But no matter how guilty he felt, he knew the duplicity must continue just a little while longer.

The waitress appeared at their booth, poured them each a cup of coffee, then took their orders and disappeared once again. "So, you told me yesterday that I came to Mustang by way of Texas. And you mentioned that your parents lived in Billings, so does that mean you're a native of Montana?''

''No. My parents originally lived in Detroit and that's where I grew up. We moved to Billings when I was fourteen. I instantly fell in love with Montana and knew this was where I wanted to spend the rest of my life.''

''It is beautiful,'' he agreed.

''As far as I'm concerned, it's the most beautiful state in the Union.'' Her eyes sparkled as she spoke and her face took on an animation that only served to increase her attractiveness. ''We lived in the city of Billings, but I'd always wanted a ranch. I was teaching fifth grade and living in an apartment when I realized unless I made some changes, I'd never be a rancher. So one weekend I took off on a round trip. The first time I drove through the dusty, sleepy town of Mustang, I knew I was home.''

Trent curled his hand around his coffee cup. The moment he'd driven through the tiny town of Mustang, he'd known this was the last place on earth Travis would choose to make his permanent home. Had he misjudged his brother? Had he discounted the positive effects of love and marriage on a man like Travis? He took a sip of his coffee, unsure what to believe.

''Were we happy?'' he asked.

His impulsive question obviously startled her. A wrinkle appeared in her brow and her hand shook slightly as she set her cup back in the saucer. ''We were adjusting.'' She smiled, but the gesture looked forced. ''You know…adapting to each other the way all newly married couples do.'' Her gaze didn't quite meet his.

Any further conversation was interrupted by the arrival of their waitress with their orders. For a few minutes they ate in silence, Trent once again analyzing the little shreds of information he'd received from her.

Something niggled at the base of his brain…an ugly supposition that refused to go away. He found it an odd coincidence that Travis had disappeared a month after Elena's trust fund had been embezzled.

He'd learned long ago never to trust coincidence where Travis was concerned. Still, he refused to contemplate all the aspects of the situation until he got an opportunity to see the ridge where Travis supposedly had fallen.

Trent looked at Elena once again. "Did we ever talk about having children?"

She smiled. This time the gesture lit her features and Trent felt a coil of warmth shoot through him in response. "One night right before we got married. You told me you wanted a whole brood of kids to fill the house. We laughed and argued because I said I wanted a little boy who looked just like you, and you wanted a little girl who looked like me. We decided we'd have half a dozen of each."

She touched her stomach, the smile slowly fading. "I thought this baby would have to be raised without a father."

She reached across the table and covered his hand with hers. Her touch was warm, her skin soft and Trent fought the need to pull away from her. "I'm so glad you're alive. They told me nobody could have survived a fall from the ridge. It's nothing short of a miracle that you're here, alive and well."

Again guilt surged up inside him and the truth battled to escape him, but he refused to let it go. Not yet. He needed to know more. Instead he gently pulled his hand from hers. "Elena, no matter what happens, I'll always be a part of the baby's life."

It was true. No matter what happened, no matter what he discovered, the child she carried was part of his family tree, a little branch that would carry not only the family blood but their name as well.

Her smile was achingly sweet. "That's what I want. A child needs a father."

Trent fought the need to explain to her he could never be the baby's father, but he could be a favorite uncle.

"You finished eating?" he asked, suddenly eager to be on the way.

"Yes, I'm finished." She set aside her napkin and together they stood to leave.

As Trent walked behind her toward the cashier, he felt a renewed urgency. The sooner he got up on that ridge, looked around and came to some conclusions, the faster he could tell Elena the truth about who he was and what minimal part he would play in her life.

The closer they got to the mountain range, the more tense Elena became. She couldn't put out of her mind the memory of that morning with Travis. He'd been cruel, more cruel than she'd ever seen him before. And yet it was difficult to resolve the memory of that man with the one who sat next to her in the car.

She shot a surreptitious glance at her husband, as always her heart beating just a tad quicker at his rugged masculinity. She was a little bit ashamed to admit that it had been his physical attractiveness that had first drawn her to him. In the months he'd been away, none of his attractiveness had diminished.

His hair was still dark and shiny, his eyes the clear

blue gray of autumn skies. His jawline was well-defined, the square chin broken by a slight cleft.

"Now *you're* staring," he said with a smile.

She felt a wave of heat steal across her cheeks, but she laughed in response. "Yes, I guess I am," she admitted. "I just still can't believe you're here...that you're alive. The park rangers and police all told me that they were certain you'd probably gone over the edge and it could be months, if ever, before the river released your body and it washed up someplace."

She looked down at her wedding ring as it glistened in the sunlight. "In the last month, I'd finally accepted that you were probably dead." *And now that you're very much alive, I don't know what to do about it,* she added silently. She wanted a father for her baby, but she couldn't forget how unhappy she'd been with Travis as her husband.

"You promised you wouldn't make me go up on the ridge. You haven't changed your mind, have you?" she asked as he pulled into the parking lot at the base of the trail that led up to the ridge.

He looked at her in surprise. "You mentioned the other day you were afraid of heights. Why would I make you do something that frightened you?"

Why indeed? He'd seemed to get a kick out of her fear that last time they had been here. She returned his gaze in confusion. "Because you made me go up there before even though you knew it scared me," she answered softly.

A muscle in his jaw knotted as he shut off the car engine, then turned to face her. "I promise, I won't ever again make you do anything that causes you fear or anxiety." He looked as if he wanted to say more, but instead he unbuckled his seat belt and opened the door. "I just follow the trail up?" he asked.

She nodded. "It will eventually take you to the ridge."

He stepped out of the car and closed the door. With a small wave, he took off walking. He even walks different, Elena thought as she watched him stride away. The Travis she remembered had swaggered in a loose-hipped gait that suggested raw sensuality.

The man walking away from her now had no hint of a swagger. His strides were long and purposeful, giving the aura of determination rather than strutting arrogance. And yet they were the same man.

Elena got out of the car, squinting against the rays of the sun to catch a glimpse of Travis as he moved up the narrow, overgrown path. Travis…and yet somehow not Travis.

Leaning against the car door, she watched until he disappeared from sight. She knew the trail wound to the other side of the tall peak and she wouldn't see him again until he made his descent.

She remembered that day just like it was yesterday. She'd sat in the car…waiting…wondering…and frantic because he hadn't returned. She'd watched not only the mouth of the trail, but any other area where he might possibly emerge, but he'd never come down. And now he was back.

She sighed and rubbed her stomach, a profusion of thoughts roiling around in her head. Was it possible for a bump on the head, a case of amnesia to completely change a man's personality? For that's what it appeared had happened.

The man who had walked into her garden the day

before seemed to have little in common with the one who had disappeared almost five months ago. How was that possible?

A wave of warmth swept through her as she thought of him telling her he'd never make her do anything that would cause her fear or anxiety. So different from the man who had bullied her up to the ridge, then had forced her to make love to him as their bodies rolled precariously close to the edge.

She turned at the sound of an approaching vehicle. A park ranger truck pulled up next to her car, a young uniformed man behind the wheel. He parked and got out, offering her a friendly smile. "Everything all right?" he asked.

"Oh, yes. I'm just waiting for my husband. He took the trail up to the top." Elena was grateful she didn't recognize the young man as one of the rangers who had been summoned when she'd raised the alarm because of Travis's disappearance.

"You're wise to wait here. It's too hot to be climbing today. You'd think we were in Arizona rather than Montana with the heat we're having this year."

Elena smiled. "Yes, it has been unusual." Her gaze went up toward the peak of the small mountain.

"The ridge up there isn't for the weakhearted. There's a steep drop off. A couple months ago we had a climber fall. Apparently the river swallowed him whole because his body hasn't been found."

Elena must have paled because the ranger smiled apologetically and got back in his truck. "Enjoy the afternoon," he said as he pulled away.

Elena once again leaned against the car door, wondering what the ranger would think if he knew she was the woman who had lost a man to the ridge, only to have him resurrected and once again climbing the mountain.

She had to figure out what she was going to do about Travis. He'd given her a perfect opportunity to open up when he'd asked if they had been happy, and she hadn't seized it.

She should have told him then that she had been unhappy and had intended to ask him for a divorce. However, something had stopped her from speaking the truth.

Compassion? After all, the man had no past. He had no place to go, no family other than her. Wouldn't it be better...kinder to tell him her plans for a divorce after he got his memory back?

And she had to admit something else...something unsettling. If she looked deep in her heart, she had to confess she was intrigued to find out if, when Travis got his memory back, he would be the same thoughtless, selfish man he had been...or would he remain this new version of himself? A man who, if she allowed herself, she just might be able to love once again.

Trent stood at the top of the ridge, his gaze scanning the landscape around him. Straight ahead across the small canyon were much higher mountain peaks, looking stark and forbidding with jagged ridges and deep shadowed areas.

Directly below, threading its way through the deep gorge was the Arganus River, the surface of the water shimmering with the play of the early afternoon sun.

Breathtaking. In every direction the landscape seemed to compete for adoration. The trail up had been narrow and at times difficult to navigate, but the view was worth every step.

He drew deep breaths of clean, sweet-scented air into his lungs, unsurprised that this had been a favorite place for his brother. From the time they had been young, Travis had loved to climb. Something about the man-versus-nature battle had drawn Travis's sense of adventure, piqued his reckless streak.

Had that reckless streak led to his death? With this question in mind, Trent directed his attention down the steep slope directly before him. If a person stumbled and fell, there was little to break the fall and in all probability, they would go down the slope and into the hungry river below.

Again he waited for a telling sense of despair, a gnawing grief to sweep over him, but it didn't come. He had no sense of Travis's death here. But he and Travis hadn't been close since they'd been small children. Would he feel his twin's death in his heart?

He narrowed his gaze, studying the vegetation that dotted the slope, the natural crevices and ravines that had been carved from wind and rain. An experienced climber could make it to the bottom.

Travis had been a skilled climber.

Trent's heart beat an uneven rhythm as he stared down toward the river.

He knew.

Deep in his gut he knew his brother was alive. Travis hadn't gone over the edge to his death. He'd climbed down and disappeared. But why?

The ugly suppositions he'd shoved away while they'd eaten breakfast returned. Was it possible Travis had something to do with Elena's missing trust fund?

"Travis, what have you done this time?" he whispered aloud.

With a sigh of regret mingling with disgust, Trent turned to make his descent. One thing was clear. He couldn't stop his subterfuge with Elena...not yet. He needed to play the part of his brother and hope he flushed out the truth. For the moment, he had to remain Elena's counterfeit husband.

Chapter 4

Elena stood at the kitchen window, staring out to the backyard where Travis worked to repair the broken corral fence. Odd. Each and every moment with this man without a memory brought surprises.

In the month they had been married Travis hadn't lifted a finger to take care of any of the repair work the place desperately needed. He'd procrastinated, then had become belligerent and angry whenever she had broached the topic of him helping out around the ranch.

He'd already gotten up and left the house before Elena got out of bed that morning. She'd found a note on the kitchen table telling her he was out looking around the place.

As she'd held the note in her hand, old emotions had resurfaced. Before the accident, Travis had often gotten up and left the ranch early, only at that time he'd never told her where he was headed or when he'd be home.

She'd spent the first month of her marriage to him with a sick feeling in her stomach, wondering exactly what she had gotten herself into by marrying him. His unexplained absences, his moodiness and secrecy hadn't been apparent before their marriage...only after.

When she'd heard the bang of a hammer, she'd run to the window, shocked to see him working on the old, rotten fencing around the corral.

He wore a faded black hat, the wide brim shading his features from the sun. The jeans that hugged his long legs were one of her favorite pairs, worn and fitted although already covered with a fine layer of Montana dust.

As he swung the hammer, banging in nails, his back expanded and the biceps beneath the short sleeved white T-shirt bulged and swelled.

Heat swept through Elena, unexpected but deliciously evocative. Oh, if only she could block out some of her memories...suffer a selective amnesia of her own making.

Her fingertips tingled with the sensory memory of caressing the planes and muscles of his back, with the memory of gripping his biceps as he made love to her.

There had been many things wrong with their marriage, but for the most part the sex had been good. Although Travis had not been a particularly tender or thoughtful lover, rarely indulging in extended foreplay, he'd been lusty and exciting.

She'd tried to adjust to his vigorous style, deciding that loving caresses and sweet romance weren't that important. But deep in her heart, she'd felt bereft when he took her quickly, then rolled over and fell asleep.

Still, there had been brief times, when he'd held her

in his arms, that she'd been able to forget her unhappiness. She wondered if this new man would make love differently. Would he stroke her languidly? Kiss her with a new gentleness? Would he hold her long after the physical act was over and it was her soul that needed caressing?

With a sigh of irritation she moved away from the window so he was no longer in her sight. She didn't want to want him again, refused to set herself up for more heartache. He might be exhibiting a different nature now, but once his memories returned, his true nature would once again be in control.

She sank down at the table, her hand automatically going to her stomach, as if to stroke the baby growing inside her. Still, she wanted Travis to have a part, not only in the child's life as it grew, but in the very process of the birth.

Elena had always believed the bonds of parenthood began not at birth, but at conception. It didn't matter that eventually she and Travis would not be a couple.

What was important was that no matter their personal relationship, they worked together to parent. Their baby needed a mother and a father to help navigate the paths of life.

She rose from the table at the sound of a car pulling up out front. Going into the living room, she peered out the window and stifled a groan. Millie Creighton. Mustang's answer to Hollywood's most successful gossip columnist.

As the older woman got out of her car, the multicolored feather plume on top of her peach-colored hat waved in the wind. Terrific. Elena swallowed another groan. If Millie was wearing a hat, then the call was business, not pleasure. She only wore a hat when she was on a gossip finding mission, seeking a little dirt to add to her weekly column in the Mustang Monitor.

Running a hand down the front of her dress, glad her hair was neatly braided, Elena drew a deep breath before she opened the door to greet Millie.

"Darling girl!" Millie swept Elena into a hug and kissed the air near Elena's cheek. She stepped back, her blue marble eyes sweeping into every nook and cranny the room had to offer, like twin vacuums seeking tiny morsels.

Her gaze returned to Elena and she clapped her hands together in obvious delight. "Oh my dear, you're positively blooming."

"Thank you," Elena returned and gestured her toward the kitchen. "Would you like a glass of soda? Perhaps some iced tea?"

"Iced tea sounds lovely," Millie agreed. She followed Elena into the kitchen and sank down at the table. "I simply had to come by and see if what I'd heard was true," she explained as Elena poured them each a glass of tea.

"It's true. Travis is back." Elena set the glasses down, then joined her at the table.

"It's news when one of the most handsome ranchers of Mustang disappear, but it's even bigger news when he suddenly reappears." Millie leaned forward, her eyes radiating blatant nosiness as her voice dropped to a stage whisper. "I hear he's not quite right in the head."

A burst of laughter escaped Elena, although she was unsurprised at the inaccurate gossip apparently making the rounds. "He's perfectly fine, although he's suffering from some sort of temporary amnesia."

Millie leaned back in her chair, obviously disappointed. "Amnesia...that's nothing. My Henry, God rest his soul, developed that whenever I ask him to run an errand for me." Millie sipped her tea thoughtfully. "So, how extensive is this temporary amnesia?"

"Pretty extensive," Elena admitted reluctantly. "But we're certain now that he's here, his memory should return fairly quickly."

"If he's suffering such a profound case of amnesia, how did he get here? What happened to him and where has he been for all these months?"

"Apparently he fell off the ridge that day and was fished out of the river by some backwoodsman. His recovery took some time and when he was finally physically able to come back here, he did. He remembered me...and this place, but little else."

Millie placed a plump hand over her heart. "Oh my, isn't that romantic? A man losing all his memories except those of his beloved wife and home." She pointed to Elena's stomach. "Your pregnancy must have been a surprise."

"It was. A very pleasant surprise." Elena refused to feed the woman anything negative. The tragedy of Travis's disappearance and the decisions Elena made now were nobody's business.

"Are you two coming to the Summerfest Dance this Friday night?" Millie asked.

Elena frowned. The Summerfest Dance was one of four big social events in the town of Mustang. She and Travis had attended the Valentine's Dance a week before he'd disappeared from the ridge. The memory of that particular dance brought a bad taste to Elena's mouth. Definitely, it had not been a pleasant night.

"I don't know…I kind of doubt it," she replied.

"I understand. You've only just got him home. I'm sure you're reluctant to share him with anyone."

Elena nodded, although that wasn't the reason she was reluctant to go to the dance. The conversation was interrupted by the opening of the back door. Travis stepped inside, his features registering surprise as he saw Millie.

"Sorry to interrupt. I didn't realize you had company," he said.

"Travis…you handsome scoundrel. It's good to see you again," Millie said, the feather in her hat bobbing with the coquettish toss of her head.

Travis smiled, his handsome features radiating bewilderment. "I'm sorry…"

"Travis, this is Millie Creighton, the social reporter for the Mustang Monitor," Elena explained pointedly.

Travis nodded his head toward Millie. "Nice to meet you, although I'm assuming we've met before since you called me a scoundrel," he said dryly. "You'll have to forgive me, I'm afraid I don't remember." He held out his hands in a gesture of helplessness.

Millie stared at him intently, puzzlement darkening the blue of her eyes. "It's all right. If you don't remember me, then thankfully you don't remember how many times I stepped on your toes at the Valentine's Dance."

He smiled. "I'm sure I didn't even notice."

Millie tipped her glass up and finished her tea, then stood. "Well, I need to get out of here. I have an appointment to interview our Summerfest Queen in fifteen minutes. I just wanted to stop by and see for myself that Travis had truly come home."

"It was nice meeting you again, Ms. Creighton," Travis said.

"Yes... Same here. It's too bad we won't be seeing you at the dance on Friday night." She grabbed Elena's arm and propelled her toward the door. "Walk me out, dear."

"He's certainly different, isn't he?" Millie said as the two women stepped outside onto the porch.

"Different? I'm not sure what you mean," Elena hedged, refusing to give fodder to the biggest mouth in Montana.

Millie shook her head, the movement displacing the hat and causing it to shift down across her gray eyebrows. She shoved it back in place with pudgy fingers, her eyes narrowed in thought. "Travis always had a certain bit of wickedness in his eyes, like life was one big joke and he was the biggest joker of all. It's not there anymore."

Elena didn't reply. In truth, she wasn't sure how to answer. Millie shrugged and gave Elena a quick hug. "Oh well, I'm sure when he gets his memory back, he'll be back to the same old scoundrel you married."

They said their goodbyes and Elena watched as Millie drove away, stirring a cloud of dust in her wake. As she watched the car disappear, she thought of Millie's parting words. Yes, eventually Travis would get his memory back and be the same old scoundrel she'd married. And that's exactly why she couldn't allow herself to feel anything for him now.

"She's quite a character," Travis said when Elena returned to the kitchen a moment later.

Elena smiled. "Only one of many the town of Mustang seems to breed. Actually, Millie has a heart of gold, but I don't think the woman could keep a secret if you sewed her mouth shut and tied her hands together. She'd somehow manage to tap out morse code with the feather in one of her ghastly hats.''

Travis laughed, a full-bodied sound that warmed her to her toes. His eyes sparkled as he gazed at her, as if she'd surprised him with her humor.

For a single moment, a bond existed between them, a shining strand of connection, an affinity of shared laughter that wrapped around Elena's heart.

She fought against it, busying herself cleaning up the glasses she and Millie had used.

"So what's this dance Millie mentioned?" he asked.

"Oh, the people of Mustang love their hoedowns. About four times a year they pull out all the stops and plan a potluck dinner and dance. This Friday night is the Summerfest celebration.''

"Did we normally go to the dances?" he asked. He leaned against the sink, so close to her she could smell his scent. An evocative odor of maleness mingling with the clean, fresh aroma of the outdoors.

"We went to one about a week before our trip to the ridge.''

"So why don't you want to go to the one Friday night?''

She frowned. Using a sponge to wipe down the table, she kept her gaze averted from him. "I don't know. The last one wasn't a particularly pleasant night.''

"I danced on your toes?''

She didn't react to his attempt at humor, the wound was suddenly too raw, too fresh to laugh about. "No, in fact, you didn't dance with me at all that night.'' She swiped at an imaginary speck on the table. "I guess my expectations were too high."

He was silent for a moment, and she felt his gaze on her, probing and intense. "You expected me to dance with my new bride? You expected me not to flirt with every other woman at the dance?"

She looked up at him sharply. "You remember that night?"

He shook his head, his eyes reflecting a haunting she didn't understand. "No, it was just a joke. But it's true, isn't it?"

"Yes, it's true. It was a horrible night."

He moved away from the sink and leaned a hip against the table. She moved from the table to the sink. "We had a terrible fight that night when we got home. I was hurt and you were angry." She shrugged. "It was my fault. I knew you were a flirt before we got married. It was part of your charm."

"A trait less charming in a husband than in a boyfriend," he observed.

"Exactly." She set her sponge down and instead picked up a dish towel, as if her hands needed something to hold.

"I think we should go to the dance Friday night." He walked over to where she stood and took the towel from her hands and set it on the counter nearby.

Something in his eyes, a soft whisper of indefinable emotion, stole her breath as he leaned closer and closer toward her. "I think we should go, and I should dance every song with my wife." With the back of his hand, he gently stroked down the curve of her cheek, along the length of her neck.

His hand was rough, dry from his work outside, but

the touch shot a shimmering wave of heat through Elena. She knew she should move away, step back from his touch, get away from the magnetic pull that threatened to sweep good sense out of her mind.

But she couldn't move…couldn't breath.

"Don't you think it would be nice to replace that unpleasant memory with a more pleasant one?" His voice was a deep, husky whisper that shot a new wave of warmth up her spine.

"Yes," she managed to sigh the assent. His lips were so close to hers all she had to do was rise up just a little and she could claim them. She could imagine their taste, the texture. Her blood heated and raced in anxious anticipation and she wet her lips with the tip of her tongue.

His eyes darkened and without warning he did what she had not been able to do…he moved away. "I'm going back outside. I'd like to finish up that fencing before dinner." His voice sounded deeper than usual with a husky undertone.

She nodded, unable to do anything else. As the screen door closed behind him, she released a sigh, unsure if the heavy expulsion of air was an expression of relief…or regret.

Trent picked up the hammer and a handful of nails, fighting off an irritation that bordered anger. The problem was he wasn't sure exactly where the anger should be directed.

It would be far too easy to focus it on Elena, whose verdant eyes had held such aching hurt when she'd spoken of the dance she and Travis had attended. A dance where her husband hadn't danced with her once and instead had flirted with all the other women in the room.

It would also be far too simple to direct his ire toward Travis. How many wounded hearts had Travis left in his wake? How many times would Trent feel obligated to sweep behind him, cleaning up messes, soothing over the chaos and pain his brother had left behind?

He swung the hammer, driving a nail nearly halfway through the new wood plank with a single blow. Finally, he found the true target for his anger. Himself.

He'd thought he'd managed to get past his feelings of responsibility where Travis was concerned. He thought he'd come to terms with the fact he was not his brother's keeper. He'd believed he no longer felt morally responsible for Travis's sins...for the pain Travis inflicted without thought.

Until he'd looked into Elena's expressive eyes.

Instantly he'd wanted to heal the wounding of her heart, soothe away that hurt and remove the pain that Travis had left behind.

He banged the nail once again, driving it the rest of the way. Tipping his hat back, he surveyed the work he'd managed to accomplish.

The rotten, broken boards had been replaced with strong, new ones, transforming the corral from a useless eyesore to a working arena. The corral now looked good and strong.

The physical labor had felt good. Trent had once dreamed of having a place like this...a ranch built with the labor of his hands and by the sweat of his brow. He'd longed for a clean and healthy place to raise a family and to sleep at night in the arms of a loving woman.

He'd once believed he'd found that woman...and Travis had destroyed those dreams.

A rhythmic pounding of hooves and a cloud of dust drew his attention to an approaching rider. He stifled a small groan as he recognized Cameron, the man's scowl as black as the horse he rode.

Cameron reined in and dismounted, his gaze on the corral. "Nice work." He turned his attention to Trent, his dark eyes displaying no hint of friendliness. "I thought you were allergic."

Trent frowned. "Allergic to what?"

"Work. You sure didn't do any before."

Trent had decided to use his time constructively while pretending to be Travis. Someplace deep in his mind, he figured it would be easier for Elena to swallow his deceit if he'd managed to fix up the place while indulging in that deceit. As if a neat and tidy ranch could ease the pain of heartbreak.

Cameron looked back at the corral. "Elena has a couple of horses at my place. I've been working with them. With the corral fixed, I can bring them over here."

Trent nodded, studying him. They stood almost the same height, Cameron perhaps an inch or so over Trent's six feet. Hostility radiated from the man, reflected in the depths of his dark eyes.

"So, what's the story on this amnesia stuff?" Cameron asked.

Trent shrugged, although his stomach tensed as he recognized the need for more lies. "No story. It's just there. We're hoping something familiar will make my memory return."

Cameron snorted. "That something familiar sure as hell won't be good, hard work. If you want something really familiar, go to the Roundup. You spent enough time there."

Trent had already decided to go to the Roundup. Just like with the decision to go to the dance on Friday night, Trent wanted to visit all Travis's haunts and maintain a high visibility. If Travis really was alive as Trent suspected, Trent knew his brother's ego alone would demand contact.

He looked back at Elena's brother. "You don't like me very much, do you?" Trent said.

Cameron took off his hat and swiped his forehead with the back of a hand. His dark eyes held Trent's gaze. "No, I don't. I didn't trust you when Elena married you and I don't trust you now."

"Then I guess it's good I didn't marry you," Trent returned dryly.

Cameron shot him a dark look of warning, obviously not the type to respond to humor. "I'll tell you one thing, Richards. Elena is a good woman, with a sweet, caring heart. When she asked me to find you after you disappeared, I have to confess, I didn't look too hard. In truth, I preferred you not be found. I had hoped you'd stay gone forever."

He slapped his hat back on his head and in one fluid motion mounted the huge black horse. "If you hurt my sister, I'll see that you pay. I'm officially not a bounty hunter anymore, but for you..." He flashed a tight smile. "I'll come out of retirement and the next time you disappear...I'll find you." Touching the horse's flanks with his heels, he took off.

Trent turned as he heard the screen door slam shut. Elena stood on the back porch. "Wasn't that Cam?" she asked.

"Yes." He dropped the hammer he'd been holding and walked over to where she stood.

"Why didn't he come in?"

"I think his reason for coming was to give me a nice brother-in-law kind of warning. He told me if I hurt you, he'd hunt me down."

Elena frowned, a delicate wrinkle appearing in the center of her forehead. "Drat that man. He's always been far too protective."

Trent said nothing, knowing in this particular case Cameron's fears were probably warranted.

"There are times I definitely feel as if I have too much big brother," she exclaimed. "I'm sorry if he offended you."

"No need to apologize for him. Being protective of those you love isn't a fault—I'd say it's quite admirable."

She tilted her head, her gaze lingering on him. She opened her mouth, as if to speak, then closed it again. Stepping off the porch, she gestured toward the corral. "Looks good."

Trent walked with her, trying not to notice the play of sun in her hair, the way the golden rays accentuated the curve of her jaw, the fullness of her lips. "Cameron mentioned a couple of horses of yours. He said now that the corral is usable, he'd be bringing them by."

She nodded, a smile curving those sensual lips. "Two weeks ago we went to an auction and I bought two mares. I got them for a song and couldn't resist, even though I really didn't have anyplace but the stables to put them. Cam agreed to keep them and work with them until he could get the corral fixed. He's got a real knack with horses." She looked at him once again, her eyes the color of deep green grass. "Thank you for your work."

Trent nodded, finding it somehow sad that she'd have to thank the man she believed her husband for fixing what needed to be fixed. "If you have any paint, I thought tomorrow I might start on painting the barn." He looked toward the gray, weathered structure.

"There's paint in the barn, along with the new wood you found for the corral." She ran a hand along the top railing of the wooden pen. "In the first few months after buying this place, I tried to get all the supplies I'd need for making it a working ranch. At that time I figured I'd have to hire someone to get the work done."

"Then we got married and you'd assumed we'd do the work together." She nodded. "But you didn't realize when you married me that I was a lazy bum."

Her eyes widened. "Is that what Cam told you?"

He grinned. "He hinted at it. But it doesn't take Einstein to figure out that I wasn't much into working around here before my accident."

"Again, perhaps my expectations of you were too high," she said softly, her gaze focused toward the distant horizon. "That seems to be a fault with me."

"I doubt it." Trent replied. She turned to look at him and in her eyes he saw confusion, bewilderment...and the whisper of an emotion that frightened the hell out of him. Hope.

"I thought maybe after dinner I'd head into town and have a couple beers at the Roundup," he said, and watched as the hope died...a glistening light snuffed out.

She nodded. "Dinner is ready," she said, and turned to head back to the house.

He watched her go, back erect with dignity. Despite what her brother probably believed, Trent had a feeling

Elena had an inner strength that her innocent, petite physical appearance belied. She was going to need it. Because he saw no way out of the fact that when this mess was cleaned up and all the facts were known, she would be hurt.

Chapter 5

"I'm going with you."

Trent released his hand from the front doorknob and turned to see Elena standing behind him. She wore jeans and a long, sleeveless tunic top that made her pregnancy seem to disappear.

She looked lovelier than he'd ever seen her, with her hair loose and skimming beyond her shoulders, and her eyes and mouth emphasized with a deft touch of makeup.

"I beg your pardon," he said, fighting against the overwhelming desire to take her in his arms, taste her rosebud lips and tangle his fingers in her glorious curtain of hair.

Twin spots of color rode high in her cheeks as she raised her chin with a touch of defiance. "To the Roundup. Before your accident, I sat home while you went there most nights. Tonight I'm going with you."

Trent wanted to protest. He intended to ask questions, seek answers, and it would be more difficult to do so with a wife at his side. But her determination shone from her eyes...lovely eyes that were shadowed with a hint of vulnerability, making it impossible for him to deny her.

"Okay, then let's go," he replied. He opened the door and gestured her out into the late evening.

The drive into Mustang was accomplished in an awkward silence, the same one that had accompanied their evening meal.

Silence was the easiest way for Trent to deal with his subterfuge. If he didn't talk, he didn't have to worry about saying something that might alert her to his deception. And yet the silence was excruciating as he found himself wanting to know all there was about her.

He wanted to know about her childhood, about the hopes she'd entertained, the dreams she'd imagined for herself. He wanted to know how she buttered her toast, if she sang in the shower.

It bothered him, this intense interest he felt growing with each day he spent with her. And what bothered him more than the interest, was the growing desire to touch her, kiss her, explore the depths of her passion with his own.

Even now, with her sitting innocently next to him, her scent eddied in the air, a mysterious blend of flowers and spice that instantly made a man think of cool sheets on a hot summer night and tangled limbs amid those sheets.

"Travis?"

"Yeah?"

"You don't remember what happened to your wedding ring?"

Trent looked at his hands on the steering wheel. A wedding ring. He hadn't considered that Travis would wear a ring. "Uh…no. I don't have any idea what happened to it. I…it must have come off during the fall or got lost somehow. I'm sorry."

"It's not your fault." Her voice held no censure, just an easy acceptance of his statement. That only added to his guilt.

He pulled into the Roundup's parking lot, the area filled with a number of cars and pickups. The building was a wooden one story, a neon cowboy with a lasso flashing on and off from the flat roof.

He jumped in surprise as Elena's hand covered his. Warm…soft…Trent responded to her touch with a swift intake of breath.

"Maybe something in here will jog your memory." Her gaze held his…a curious blend of hope and anxiety. "You spent a lot of time here. Didn't the doctor say familiar places and people will eventually give you back your memories?"

He nodded, wishing she'd keep her hand over his forever, wishing she'd remove it as soon as possible. He opened his car door. "I guess we won't find out by sitting here in the car."

As they walked together toward the front door, Trent wondered why she'd looked just a little bit afraid at the prospect of him getting his memories back.

Didn't she want her husband back as a whole man? With the memories of their brief marriage? He quickly decided he'd misread her expression, certain that she wanted his memory back more than anyone.

The moment he opened the door and stepped inside, Trent felt as if he'd entered his brother's den. Smoke greeted them, along with the pounding of bass from the jukebox and the clink of glasses from the bar. Excited shouts and the hollow sound of a cue stick hitting balls radiated from the back where several pool tables were being used.

Yes, this was a place where Travis would have felt at home...amid the chaos and the abundance of flesh displayed by the skimpily clad waitresses.

"Hey, Travis!" The bartender grinned widely and waved them toward two bar stools. He high-fived Trent. "Good to see you back, man. We all thought we'd never see you again." He turned his attention to Elena, his eyebrows raised in surprise. "Hi, Elena. First time in here for you, isn't it?"

"Hi, Sam. Yes...first time." She slid onto one of the empty stools, looking as out of place as a flower blooming in a garbage pile.

"What can I get you, sweets?" Sam asked her.

"Club soda with a twist of lime."

He nodded and looked back at Trent. "The usual?"

"Fine." Trent sat down next to Elena and twisted around to view the surroundings. The place was a dive. Not the worst Trent had ever been in, but definitely a place that didn't cater to the upper crust of Mustang.

The floor was covered with sawdust except for a small area where couples two-stepped to the country music. The crowd was raucous. Bawdy laughter and whisky-laden voices rose and fell in the peculiar rhythm of bar life.

"Here you are," Sam said as he set a club soda in front of Elena and a glass of amber liquid before Trent.

"I'll just put it on your tab," he said, then moved down the bar to attend to another customer.

"I can't believe you liked to come in here," Elena said softly as the jukebox momentarily fell silent.

"Yeah, I'm having problems believing it myself," he replied. He took a sip of his drink and tried not to grimace. He'd forgotten Travis's drink of choice was cheap scotch. Trent hated scotch.

"It's just so...so...frenzied," Elena observed.

"Travis...sweetheart!"

Trent nearly fell off his stool as one of the waitresses wound her arms around his neck and planted a kiss on his cheek. She released him and stepped back, her blue eyes sparkling with friendliness. "I heard you were back, but I told everyone I wouldn't believe it until I saw you in here."

She whipped her head around, her shoulder-length blond hair flying as she focused on Elena. "Hi, Elena...bet you're glad to have him back. All the waitresses in here had a party when we heard Travis was back. He's the best tipper this dump has ever seen."

"Hey, Amanda...you working or what?" A patron called from across the room.

"Oops, gotta run." With a quick smile, she whirled around, the short cowgirl skirt exposing a long length of leg as she hurried toward the customer.

"At least I didn't have the reputation as a cheapskate," he observed. He looked back at the waitress, wondering exactly what her relationship had been with Travis. Had it merely been waitress and patron? "Amanda who?"

"Amanda Creighton. Millie's daughter," Elena said. She smiled at Trent's expression of surprise. "I know…it's a shock, isn't it? From what I understand, Amanda and her mom had some sort of falling out about a year ago. Amanda moved out, and since then she and her mom don't speak.''

Trent looked back over to the pretty blonde. Hard to believe the flirtatious waitress was the daughter of the socialite gossipmonger. And yet not so hard to believe.

Trent had learned firsthand about rebellion from a master…his brother. Travis had rebelled against their parents, against his brother and against society. What Trent was determined to find out was just how far Travis had taken his rebellion.

As he and Elena sat sipping their drinks, Elena whispered to him names and occupations of the patrons in the bar. Each time she leaned toward him to share a snippet of information, he caught a whiff of her perfume. The scent muddied his senses, made it difficult to focus on the reason he'd come here.

"No memories?" She asked, her eyes luminous in the dim lighting.

"None," he replied, and thought he saw a flash of relief cross her features. He frowned thoughtfully and signaled Sam for more ice in his drink. Surely he was misreading her. It just didn't make sense that she wouldn't want him to retrieve his lost memories.

"Excuse me for a minute," she said as she slid off the stool. "I'll be right back."

Trent watched her make her way through the crowd toward the back of the bar where a sign pointed to the location of the restrooms. Her hips swayed gracefully with each step, an unconscious invitation. Trent felt the blood in his veins heat and flow faster as his gaze lingered on her.

Something about her stoked a hunger inside him. Distinctly unsettling and more than a little shameful. She was his brother's wife...carrying his brother's child. And perhaps that's why you want her, a little voice whispered inside his brain.

He wrapped his fingers around his cool glass. Elena belonged to Travis, and Travis had often taken pleasure in taking what was Trent's. Maybe it was a perverse need to pay back that fed Trent's attraction to Elena. Ugly...but possible.

He smiled tersely as Sam sidled up across the bar from him. "Heard you have some kind of amnesia." Sam wiped the inside of a glass with a towel.

"You heard right," Trent replied.

Sam sighed. "Guess that means you don't remember the name or the phone number of that cute little blonde you were meeting in my back room for a while."

Adrenaline shot through Trent. "Cute little blonde?"

"Yeah. You met with her a couple of times before you married Elena. I figured if you weren't interested in her anymore, then maybe you wouldn't mind...you know...her and me..." Sam smiled sheepishly.

"You don't know her name?"

Sam shook his head. "Never heard you mention it, although I know she wasn't from Mustang. She was a sharp dresser, sort of, you know, sophisticated looking." Sam frowned. "Doesn't ring a bell, huh. You met her twice...no, three times in my back room. Told me to keep it hush-hush."

"And this was before I married Elena?" Trent asked.

Sam nodded. "I think it was before you even met Elena. I asked you at the time if it was business or pleasure and you grinned and told me a little bit of both." Sam shrugged. "Oh well, just thought I'd give it a try. Cute little blondes…they sort of ring my bell, if you know what I mean."

"Afraid I can't help you. I just don't remember." Trent's head spun with this new information…information he sensed was important, but was unsure what to make of it.

A cute little blonde…business and pleasure. "Sam, how long before I met Elena was I meeting this woman?" he asked.

Sam leaned forward on the counter, his brow wrinkled thoughtfully. "Oh, I'm not sure…maybe a couple of weeks or so. Seems to me you met her for the last time right around Thanksgiving, and by Christmas time I heard you and Elena were an item."

"Has the blonde been back in here since then?"

Sam shook his head. "Nah, haven't seen her since I saw her with you." He straightened and cleared his throat, his gaze signaling Elena's approach. "Can I get you another one of those, Elena?" he asked as he pointed to her empty glass.

"No, thanks, I'm fine."

Trent stood. "This isn't working," he said. "Nothing seems familiar at all. We might as well go on home."

"Okay…if you're ready, I am," she agreed.

Together they walked out of the bar and into the fresh, clean night air. "Oh, that's much better," Elena said, drawing a deep breath.

A stab of guilt arrowed through Trent. "Oh, God, I didn't even think about how bad the smoke in there might be for you. Are you all right?" He took her by the elbow, damning himself for his thoughtlessness. He should have insisted she remain at home. She had no business hanging out in a smoke-filled haunt in her condition.

She stopped walking and turned toward him. "I'm fine. Although I wouldn't want to stay in there for long periods of time." A soft smile curved her lips and she placed a palm against his cheek. "But thanks for caring." She dropped her hand and they continued walking toward the car.

Beneath the vaporous lamp that illuminated the parking area, she paused, her eyes widening as she grabbed for Trent's hand. "Oh…" Without warning, she pressed his hand against her tummy. "Oh, Travis…can you feel that?"

He did. Beneath his palm, he felt the fluttering of life, the stir of the babe within her. Awe swooped through him, a wondrous awe that brought emotion thick into his throat.

For just a moment as they stood intimately close together, his hand pressed firmly against her swollen stomach, it was as if they were two parents, bonded physically and spiritually by the utter miracle of a life they had created.

"The…the baby," he finally stuttered, like a man just discovering the gift of language.

Elena laughed, her eyes glittering brightly. "Yes. Our baby," she replied. She laughed again, the sound sending shivers of desire up Trent's spine. "He's definitely going to be a gymnast. He's already got the somersaults down pat."

"He?" Trent moved his hand away reluctantly, savoring the lingering miraculous feel of life.

"Or she." Elena stepped back from him and the light

of joy in her eyes faded. The moment of unencumbered connection between them was broken.

Trent knew in her mind his amnesia stood as a barrier to a normal relationship. She had no idea the biggest obstruction of all was that he wasn't the man she thought him to be. He wasn't her husband. He wasn't Travis. And he couldn't tell her the truth. Not yet. He had to find out who the blonde was and what, if anything, she knew about Travis's disappearance.

Elena stared at herself in her dresser mirror and smoothed a hand down the front of her dress. It was ridiculous to feel so nervous about going to a dance with her husband. And yet, she'd been nervous for the last week, ever since he'd returned to her life.

For the first several nights he'd been home, she'd lay in bed, watching her bedroom door. She'd been certain that somehow in the hours of the night his memory would return and he'd barge into her bedroom to claim his husbandly rights. But that hadn't happened.

There had been moments, split seconds in which she'd thought she saw a gleam of desire light his eyes, but he hadn't attempted any real physical contact.

She saw the confusion that muddied her eyes, felt that same confusion swirl within her. What did she want from Travis? Why did she long for him to take her into his arms, kiss her until her mind spun dizzily? Why did she yearn for his touch? Want him to make love to her?

Turning away from the mirror, she emitted a sigh of irritation. The problem was, she didn't want Travis to do all that...at least not the Travis she had known before his accident. She wanted the Travis who lived with her now, the man without memories, the man who treated her with gentleness and respect.

"Elena?" A soft knock fell on her bedroom door. "Are you ready?"

"I'll be out in a minute," she replied, nerves once again tingling through her body. Her heart had been broken in dozens of pieces by the man she had married, and now that same man seemed to be working hard to fit those shattered pieces back together again. But how could she trust him not to break her heart again?

With a deep sigh, she eyed her reflection one last time. She'd only gained ten pounds so far with her pregnancy, the extra pounds were carried like a small basketball low in her belly. So far, despite being five months pregnant, she hadn't had to resort to maternity clothes, but still managed to wear loose-fitting dresses that accommodated the extra weight.

The dress she wore now was a multicolored swirl of fabric, high waisted and falling to her ankles. The bright colors emphasized her dark coloring and gave her a gypsylike appearance.

For just a moment, she remembered the last dance, her humiliation as she'd leaned against the wall and watched her new husband flirt and dance and laugh with every woman in the room except her. She'd sensed looks of pity directed her way and her embarrassment had grown like a ravaging cancer.

"Don't let it be the same way tonight," she whispered to her reflection, then turned and left the room.

She found Trent in the living room. He stood at the window, staring out into the dark of the night. He turned to face her and she saw the flare of pleasure in his eyes.

"Wow...you look great!" he exclaimed.

"You don't look so bad yourself, cowboy," she returned. In truth, he looked devastatingly handsome. Pale blue jeans hugged his long legs, emphasizing muscular thighs and his slender waist. The dark blue shirt sported pale pearl buttons and western stitching in light blue thread. A small silver buckle rode the belt at his waist, his initials engraved in script lettering.

"Shall we go?"

"Just let me get the salad I made for the potluck dinner," she said, remembering the dish she was taking to the dance. It took her only a moment to get the large bowl from the refrigerator. When she returned, Travis took the bowl from her, then guided her out of the house with his hand lightly touching the small of her back.

"It's a beautiful night," he said a moment later as they headed toward Mustang.

"Gorgeous," she agreed. The unusual hot spell had snapped and the last couple of days had been comfortably warm, with cooler, pleasant nights.

"It's definitely nicer to paint when it's cooler."

She nodded. For the past two days he'd spent most of his time painting the barn. She'd watched him working for long periods, trying to understand how amnesia could transform a man so completely.

And every night she worked hard to guard her heart against this new man, who she knew at any moment could regain his memory and once again become his former self.

"You need to turn left at the corner to get to the community center," she said as they approached the one and only traffic light in town.

Before they even reached the community center, it was apparent that this night was a special night in the town of Mustang. Couples and whole families dotted the sidewalks, all walking in the same direction. The women carried covered dishes and everyone looked as if they had been spit shined for the occasion.

As Travis angled their car into a parking space in front of the community center, Elena tensed in nervous anticipation.

Perhaps here, Travis would regain his memory. The whole town would turn out for the dance. Maybe somebody's face would jog his memory, or a song that the band played. Who knew what small catalyst might stimulate the part of his brain where his memories were hidden? And then what? And then she'd have to make decisions and choices that would affect the rest of her life.

"You okay?" Travis asked with concern.

"I'm fine." She forced a smile. What else could she tell him? That she was afraid he'd regain his memory and become a man she could no longer love?

"Good." He returned her smile warmly. "Then let's go inside and have a wonderful evening."

The community center had been decorated especially for the dance. Bright-colored streamers cascaded from balloon bouquets and hung down from the ceiling and walls and on the stage at one end of the hall, the band members warmed up, their instruments squeaking and groaning as they twiddled and tuned.

Two long tables were laden with food, savory dishes whose scents wafted in the air. Travis placed the salad on one of the tables, then took Elena's arm and guided her toward the chairs lined up against the wall.

"Would you like something to drink?" he asked.

"No, thanks. I'm fine for now." She felt herself relaxing beneath his solicitous attention. She wanted to relax, have a good time.

There had been too much tension, too much uncomfortable awkwardness between them for the last week. And for the past week her head had spun with too much confusion. Tonight she didn't want to think. She simply wanted to enjoy this new man who was her husband.

He eased into the chair next to her, bringing with him the heady scent of minty soap and the earthy spice cologne she found so appealing.

For the next few minutes, as people arrived and the community center filled, Elena and Travis were greeted by fellow townspeople. When each group left, Elena quickly whispered to Travis the names and relationships of the people he'd forgotten.

"Oh my...how nice. You decided to come after all." Millie's strident voice rose in the air and the crowd parted before her like the Red Sea for Moses. Travis stood as she approached, a purple plume quivering atop her hat like a divining stick.

"Hello, Mrs. Creighton. Nice to see you again," he said.

She smiled and reached up to pat his cheek. "Millie, dear boy. You always call me Millie." She gazed at Elena, her expression friendly and openly curious. "You look lovely tonight, my dear. I can see that having your handsome husband back has put color into your cheeks."

She looked back at Travis. "I was so worried about her, out there on the ranch all alone in her condition. Now, the important question...are you going to save a dance for me this evening?" She tilted her head and cast Travis a coy smile.

"I'm afraid not. I've promised all my dances tonight to Elena."

Millie looked startled, then smiled with approval. "I don't know what happened to you, Travis Richards, but that knock on your head or whatever seems to have given you some character." Millie's gaze left him and darted to a small crowd standing nearby. "Oh, got to run. There's Wilma Casey."

She leaned closer to Travis and Elena and lowered her voice. "I hear she's having a torrid affair with Bill Riley down at the feed store. I need to check it out." As she hurried away, the plume bobbed and waved, as if emitting silent warning signals that Millie was on the prowl.

"Whew." Travis sank back down next to Elena. "She kind of gives the impression that she's taking all the oxygen out of the air."

Elena laughed. "I don't think she's ever off-duty. Millie doesn't know the meaning of 'off the record.'"

"So, when does the music start?" Travis asked.

"We'll eat first, then the band will start to play," Elena explained. "That's about the time the men start sneaking out into the parking lot to nip at Tom Mathews' home brew."

Travis smiled, his gaze holding hers for a long moment. "I think that's part of the evening activities that I'll skip."

Within minutes, the crowd surged toward the tables, indicating that the potluck dinner had officially begun. Travis and Elena got in line and when they arrived at the tables, they each filled their plates to near-overflowing capacity.

"I always overeat at these things," Elena said as she

tried to decide if the casserole she was eating was chicken or tuna.

"I've never seen so much food," Travis said.

"That's one of the nicest things about the people of Mustang. They're very generous and giving."

"You love it here, don't you?"

She nodded. "Like I told you the other day, this is my home. In the weeks after you disappeared, dozens of people stopped by to make sure I was all right, that I didn't need anything. Mustang is a town with a big heart."

Again his gaze held hers. "I have a feeling the people of Mustang embraced you because you have a heart as big as theirs."

She flushed and concentrated on her dinner, warmed by his words and by the softness his gaze held. Oh, this man was touching her in places he'd never reached before.

For the rest of the meal, their conversation was kept light and easy, often interrupted by greetings from friends and neighbors. Kids raced around the room, mothers hollering for them to sit down and eat, and laughter filled the air as the people of Mustang enjoyed the good food and one another's company.

When the meal was finished, Elena helped the women clear off tables and throw away paper plates and cups. As she worked, Travis meandered across the room to join a group of other ranchers, who appeared to be discussing the price of beef.

As she worked, Elena couldn't help but notice how tall, how handsome he looked as he joined into the conversation, his features lit with animation. The baby kicked and she gently pressed a hand against her stomach.

She had been so certain that day on the ridge, had known that her only course of action was to divorce Travis. She'd been so unhappy with their marriage, so unhappy with him. But since he'd returned, things were so different. He was so different. And suddenly her decision concerning the divorce didn't feel quite so conclusive.

Chapter 6

Trent tried to concentrate on the conversation surrounding him...conversation centering on crops, cattle and weather patterns. But it was difficult to focus on the men when his gaze was continually drawn to Elena.

Elena, who looked like a sparkling rainbow in her multicolored dress. Elena, who smelled like a spring day filled with fragrant flowers.

It was obvious she was well liked by her neighbors and fellow townspeople. As she helped clean up the potluck mess, he noticed that she was stopped and greeted often, embraced in quick hugs by many of the other women.

At least she would have plenty of support around her when all the facts came to light and she found herself alone, he thought. But this thought brought him little comfort. She wouldn't be alone. She'd have a newborn baby...a baby without a father. There would be no father to play catch, no daddy to kiss good-night. For even if Travis was found alive and well, Trent knew his brother wouldn't want to bother with the demands of a wife and child.

Without warning, the band launched into a rousing tune, a favorite line dance that instantly had people scrambling for position on the sawdust covered dance floor.

The small group of men Trent had been visiting with broke up, some joining their wives on the dance floor and others drifting toward the back door, presumably to nip a little home brew.

Trent, seeing that Elena was still occupied, sat in a chair against the wall and divided his attention between the dancers and Elena.

He smiled, fully relaxing for the first time in a week, as he watched the enthusiastic, but sometimes clumsy movements of the dancers. Laughter mingled with the music as people misstepped, lost the rhythm, and destroyed the synchronism of the group. It quickly became apparent that style wasn't important, nor was doing the line dance correctly. The whole point seemed to be to have fun.

He looked over to Elena, who'd paused in her work and also watched the dancers. Her face was lit with a smile and her foot tapped the cadence of the song.

Her gaze moved, connected with his and for a long moment held. Her smile deepened, softened as if especially for him. As if he'd been sucker punched, Trent felt he couldn't draw in enough air.

Her smile, unguarded and open, suggested intimacy, implied a sweet yearning that stoked desire inside

Trent's veins. Heat began at his toes and rose, warming his insides with a yearning of his own.

He jerked his gaze away from hers, breaking the connection as he drew a deep breath. How could Travis just walk away from a woman like Elena? Surely only death could be the reason for his absence from her. And yet, he still didn't believe Travis was dead.

Standing up, he drew in another gulp of air. He had to tell her the truth. He had to tell her he wasn't Travis, that her husband hadn't miraculously returned to her life. Tonight he'd tell her. After the dance when they were alone. He'd give her tonight to live in the fantasy, then he would shatter that fantasy and hope she didn't hate him too much for his deception.

The band eased into a slow, romantic song. Husbands and wives sought each other's arms, lovers fell together and Trent sought Elena. The slow dance was a perfect excuse to hold her in his arms before he irrevocably separated himself from her.

He found her in the kitchen washing her hands. "You ready to kick up your heels on the dance floor?" he asked.

Her face lit, eyes shining with pleasure. She nodded and quickly dried her hands. Together they left the small kitchen and moved toward the other couples who moved and swayed to the slow beat.

She fit perfectly against him, the top of her head brushing the underside of his jaw. She displayed no shyness, no hesitancy, but rather molded herself to him, allowing her breasts to press against his chest, the slight swell of her stomach to nestle into his lower abdomen.

Trent had to remind himself to move his feet, as all he really wanted to do was stand and hold her. Her hands on his shoulders radiated heat through his shirt material and her breath, warm and sweet, caressed the hollow of his neck.

Again, the heat of desire warmed his blood. His pulse quickened and he wasn't sure the pounding heart he heard was his own, or hers. "Are you having a good time?" he asked, needing conversation to take his mind off the sensual swirl of desire.

She inched back to look up at him. "Yes. I'd forgotten how much I enjoy these quarterly get-togethers. We all get so busy with our own lives, it's nice to take a night to catch up with friends and neighbors."

He nodded, grateful for the slight distance she'd placed between their bodies. "Your brother certainly doesn't look too thrilled to be here." He nodded his head in the direction where Cameron sat alone, looking unapproachable and distant.

Elena shot a glance at her brother, then looked back up at Trent. "Cam keeps himself too isolated. What he really needs is a special woman in his life."

"Don't tell me you're one of those hopeless romantics who believe love conquers all," he teased.

She frowned, her eyes darkening with a whisper of disillusionment. "I used to believe that. I'm not sure what to believe anymore." She said no more, but instead moved back against him, her face once again hidden in the front of his shirt.

Trent's heart constricted. Damn you, Travis, he thought as he tightened his arms around his brother's wife. Damn you for hurting this woman, for stealing dreams and destroying illusions of love and happily-ever-after.

The next song was a two-step and after that another

line dance. Elena's eyes glowed with laughter as he gamely tried to maneuver the unfamiliar steps. She was a woman born for laughter. Her cheeks were pinkened, and her features radiated overwhelming beauty as mirth filled her. The sound of her low, melodic giggles rode through him like sweet music on a breeze. And he wished he could keep the sparkle in her eyes, the laughter on her lips for the rest of her life.

As a new song began, the music once again slow…languid, she moved back into his arms. Her body felt like liquid heat as it pressed against…into his own.

Despite his intentions to the contrary, Travis felt himself responding. Without volition, his hands caressed up and down her back, felt the heat of her skin through the thin dress. His heartbeat accelerated, sending blood surging through him.

He knew his body was betraying him, knew she would be able to feel his desire and yet he could do nothing to stop the swell of blood that filled his veins.

She moved her hips…just a slight movement. At the same time her arms tightened around his neck, letting him know she knew he desired her, and the feeling was returned.

And why wouldn't it be? She thought him to be her husband. Why shouldn't she encourage his desire? In truth, he'd been surprised she hadn't invited him back into their bed yet.

She raised her head to look at him, her eyes brilliant, lips parted. He knew she wanted him to kiss her, saw her need shining in her eyes. And he couldn't deny her this one simple thing.

He lowered his lips and touched hers, instantly recognizing there was nothing simple about kissing Elena.

Her lips contained the heat of a stormy summer night, the sizzle of lightning renting the sky. Her tongue touched his and his heart exploded with a thunderous pounding. He drank deeply of her, momentarily getting lost in the tempest of her kiss.

Before all rational thought left him, while he still had the ability to think, he ended the kiss. "I believe this is a family gathering," he said, unsurprised that his voice was shaky with suppressed emotion.

She laughed, her cheeks stained a becoming pink. "Sorry...it's just...it's just been so long." Her voice held a quivering tone as well. She stepped back from him. "I think I'll go get a cup of punch," she said.

He dropped his arms from around her. "And I think I'll step outside for a breath of fresh air." He watched her cross the floor to the table where a smiling, older woman was serving punch, then he turned and headed out the door.

Stepping outside into the sweet night air, he drew a deep breath, trying to rid himself of the desire that still burned in his veins.

Desire.

Desire for his brother's wife. He drew both hands down his face, a ragged sigh escaping him. What kind of man was he? A man like Travis? Who took what he wanted without regard of consequences or propriety?

No, he wasn't like his brother. But he recognized the possibility that his wanting Elena was really the need to pay Travis back for his betrayal of Trent. With Joyce.

Trent leaned against the building, away from the door where people milled about. Joyce. Funny how thoughts of her no longer hurt. Perhaps Travis had done him a favor in seducing the woman Trent had meant to make his bride. Maybe she hadn't been right for Trent after all.

He shoved thoughts of the past away. He couldn't focus on old baggage, on history. He had enough problems to deal with right here in the present.

He had to tell Elena the truth. He had to confess to her his true identity. Tonight. Before things flared out of control. He wasn't sure if his desire for her was a natural emotion, or an emotion more insidious, bred in anger and the need for revenge. In any case, it didn't matter.

"Are you Travis?" a thin, childish voice drew him from his inner turmoil.

He looked down to see a young red-haired boy standing before him. "Yeah, I'm Travis."

The boy held out a folded piece of paper. "The lady said to give you this. Said you'd give me a dollar."

Trent dug into his pocket and pulled out a rumpled dollar bill. They made the exchange and Trent opened the note. As he read the printed words, adrenaline soared through him.

Travis, you double-crossing snake! Meet me Monday night at midnight in the usual place. Bring the money!!!

Trent bent down and eyed the boy solemnly. "I'll give you another dollar if you tell me where the lady was when she gave you this note and what she looked like." He pulled out another dollar and gave it to the boy.

"She was pretty," he said with a shy smile. "She had short yellow hair and was wearing black pants and a white shirt. She give me the note out in the back parking lot." He frowned worriedly. "You won't tell my ma I was out there, will you?"

Trent stood quickly. "No, I won't tell your ma," he said as he took off running toward the back of the building.

Directly behind the building, a group of men stood around, sipping from jugs that Trent assumed held the home brew. "Hey, Travis, come have a nip," one of them shouted as he flew past.

"Not now." The parking lot was full of cars and trucks. The single pole light in the center of the lot blinked and flashed as if ready to short out at any moment. Trent raced from row to row, searching...seeking the mysterious woman who had made contact.

He found two teenagers making out in the back of a car. Between two trucks near the light pole, a group of young boys ogled a skin magazine probably pilfered from a father's dresser drawer. But there was no shorthaired blonde anywhere to be seen.

"Damn." He cursed soundly as he made his way back toward the building.

Whoever she was, she was gone now. Disappeared like a ghost...a phantom. He knew there had been no shorthaired blonde in black slacks and white blouse at the dance. She'd come specifically to see that he got the note. He pulled the note from his pocket and read it again.

The usual place. He frowned. Where in the hell was the usual place? The back room of the Roundup? The young boy had described the same woman Travis had met several times at the Roundup. Who was she and where did she fit into Travis's disappearance?

There was no way he could tell Elena the truth now. At least not yet. Not when he'd managed to flush out a new player to whatever game Travis might be playing.

Right now Elena treated him like Travis because she believed him to be Travis. If he told her the truth, her reactions to him would change, and somebody might sense the difference. Or she might confide in somebody the truth, and in a town this size, there were few confidences that would be kept.

He simply couldn't take that chance. Not now. As difficult as it might get, he had to keep up his deception.

It was nearly eleven o'clock when Trent asked if Elena was ready to call it a night. She was. It had been a pleasant evening, but she'd had enough dancing and visiting for one night. What she wanted was some time alone with her husband.

As they drove home, she leaned her head back and replayed the evening in her mind. Travis had been like a fantasy come true. He'd been attentive and solicitous, displaying all the qualities that had first made her fall in love with him.

She opened an eye and snuck a peek at him. His hair was slightly mussed from the night's activities. His shirt was wrinkled and his lower jaw sported the beginning of a five o'clock shadow, and Elena had never wanted him more in her life.

"Tired?" he asked as he pulled into their driveway.

"A little. Mostly I was tired of the noise. After ten o'clock the noise level always seems to rise at those gatherings."

He parked the car and they got out. As they climbed the porch steps, Elena gestured to the two chairs. "Want to sit for a little while? It's a beautiful night and I'm too wound up to sleep.''

"All right," he agreed. He eased down into one of the wicker chairs and Elena sank into the other one.

The real reason she'd wanted to sit out here was because she wasn't ready for the night to end. She knew when they went inside he would go to the spare room and she would go into the master bedroom, into a bed lonely and cold.

She wanted just a few more minutes of his company, a few more minutes of an evening that had chased away the bad memories of the previous dance they had attended. She wanted, just for tonight, to believe that he was the man she'd fallen in love with, not the man he'd become after the wedding ceremony.

"The moon looks so low, like you could reach up and pluck it right out of the sky," he observed.

She smiled. "When my family first moved to Montana, that's the first thing I noticed, that the Montana moon seemed bigger, brighter and closer than the one in Detroit.'' She wrapped her arms around her shoulders. "I fell in love with the Montana moon first...then the land.''

"It is beautiful," he agreed.

"My dad used to say that if he could live anywhere in the world, he'd live here. He said God's stamp of approval was on every single acre in the state.''

Trent smiled, his features visible in the strong moonlight. "He sounds like a nice man.''

"He was. He and my mother were good people.''

"You miss them.''

She nodded and sighed, a wave of grief stealing over her.

"Did I meet them?"

"No. They'd been gone almost two months when I first met you." She stared up at the stars, remembering that time of mourning. Travis had eased her pain, making her find her laughter once again, sweeping her up on wings of passion that had soothed her grief.

"What does Lydia Walsh look like?"

She startled and turned her gaze on him in surprise. "Why do you want to know?"

He shrugged, his face displaying no emotion that she could discern. "Just curious. She stole your inheritance, and I'd just like to know what the woman looks like."

Although his reasoning really didn't make sense to Elena, she couldn't imagine anything but curiosity prompting his question. "She's about thirty. Thin, with short blond hair and delicate features. She's quite attractive." She frowned. "I would think it would be difficult for a woman who looks like her to just disappear. She's too pretty to blend into a crowd. But she's certainly been successful at covering her tracks."

Trent stood. "I think I'm going to call it a night," he said.

She rose also, touching his arm to stop him before he could enter the house. "Travis, thank you for tonight. I had a lovely time. Truly one of the best I can remember."

He smiled. "One of the best I remember as well."

She laughed. "That's not saying much considering you have amnesia."

"Even without all my memories, I know tonight was one of my best." He touched her cheek lightly. "I'm going to bed. Goodnight, Elena." With that, he entered the house and disappeared down the hallway toward his room.

Elena followed more slowly, her cheek burning where he'd made contact. She let Spooky out for a brief romp before bed, then called the poodle back inside.

She closed the front door and locked it, her mind replaying the kiss they had shared. Funny, he even kissed differently now.

Before, Travis's kisses had been almost punishing, hard enough that she often felt her lips had been bruised. This time, his lips had been featherlight against hers. Even when the kiss had deepened, he'd remained gentle...tender, touching desires, stoking dreams she'd believed long forgotten.

She made her way into her bedroom and changed from her dress to her nightgown. She turned out the light then crawled beneath the cool, crisp sheets. A warm summer night breeze drifted in the window, bringing with it the fragrance of sweet wild flowers, rich dark earth and plush green fields.

Spooky jumped up on the bed and curled into her usual place at the foot of the bed. Travis had refused to allow Spooky a place in the bed. It was only after he'd disappeared that Elena had allowed the dog to sleep with her.

Rolling over on her back, she stared up at the ceiling, her thoughts consumed by the man in the room across the hall. Travis. Her husband. The man whom months before she'd decided to divorce, but now had fallen in love with all over again.

Heat swept through her as she remembered those moments on the dance floor...moments when she'd known he desired her, had felt the evidence of that desire pressing against her. And she'd wanted him. Still wanted him.

So why wasn't he in here with her? Why hadn't he tried to follow through on what had begun on the dance floor when they'd returned home? She turned on her side, wondering if he were lying in bed thinking the same thoughts. Was it possible he was waiting for her to make the first move?

Before she was fully conscious of her actions, she'd left her bed and stood poised at her bedroom door. She paused, hand on the knob, aware that the choice she made now was as important as any she'd ever made before.

If she made love with Travis tonight, she was inviting him back into her life, back into her heart. Did she want to do that? Did she want to risk loving a man with no memories, knowing with foresight that when he retrieved those missing memories he might once again revert back to a man she'd find impossible to love?

Heat once again shimmered through her. She didn't want to worry about what the future might hold. Tonight she simply wanted to be with her husband. She turned the doorknob and stepped out into the dark hallway. The spare room was right across from hers and she stood just outside the door, her heart pounding like thunder.

A lingering hesitation gnawed at her as she remembered the last time they'd made love…how he'd forced her, how he'd laughed when he'd rolled them toward the edge of the ridge and she had screamed and clutched at him.

The memory surged inside her, ugly and painful. She shoved it aside, refusing to think about it. Besides, she knew the man who'd walked through her gate over a week ago, the man she'd danced with this evening, wasn't capable of that kind of behavior. It made no sense, but somehow the man fate had returned to her had lost the behaviors and personality traits she'd grown to hate.

With a hand that trembled slightly, she opened the door. Moonlight streamed into his window and she could see him lying on top of the sheets, clad only in a pair of boxers.

"Elena?" He sat up. "Is everything all right?"

"Yes. I just...I wanted..." Her voice trailed off. She wasn't accustomed to seduction. Travis had always been the one to initiate their lovemaking. She walked over to the edge of his bed. "Could you just hold me for a little while?"

She didn't give him an opportunity to reply. She slid onto the bed next to him and wrapped her arms around his bare chest. His scent, familiar and yet subtly different surrounded her, caused waves of heat to once again suffuse her.

"Elena..."

"Please, Travis. I know this last week has been difficult on you, not having your memories. I just want to be held by my husband for a little while." She raised her head to look at him. "Is that so wrong?"

She saw his hesitation in the glow of his eyes, felt the tension that tightened his muscles. With a slight groan, he closed his eyes and wrapped her in his arms. "No...no, it isn't wrong," he whispered.

Elena buried her face in the hollow of his throat as her hands stroked up and down his warm, muscled back. He held her gently, as if she were a precious, fragile gift. His hands caressed down her back gently... tentatively, yet igniting flames each place they stroked.

This was what Elena had once dreamed about...a strong man holding her, making her feel safe and loved. Before, whenever Travis had held her, it had been with impatience.

But tonight, he seemed content just to hold her. There was no impatient urgency to his caresses. But Elena felt an urgency growing inside of her.

She moved her legs against his, her nightgown riding up, allowing her to feel the tactile pleasure of his skin against hers. She pressed a kiss into the hollow of his throat where his pulse beat rapidly. A low moan escaped him.

She raised her head, seeking his lips, wanting him to kiss her until she was mindless with passion. His mouth claimed hers hungrily as his hands tangled in her hair.

The kiss stole her breath, but it was as if he breathed for her. She felt his heartbeat against her own, the rhythms matching until they blended into one. One heart. One body. Desire swirled in her head, casting away all thoughts of the past, all doubts of this man. At least for this moment, she loved him and more than anything she wanted to make love with him.

She gasped as his hands moved from her hair, down to her breasts, touching her through the thin material of her gown. She ripped at the tiny buttons, wanting to rid herself of the barrier that kept his flesh from hers. He slid his hands into the opening she created. He cupped her breasts with hot hands as his mouth continued to possess hers.

He rolled them over, so she was beneath him and she

automatically arched up to move her hips against his.
His mouth left hers, trailing a blaze down her throat and
past her collar bone. She cried out as his tongue flicked
across the peaks of her breasts, sending shivers of desire
through her.

"Travis...make love to me," she moaned, her hands
gripping his taut biceps to pull him closer...closer still.

Abruptly he swung off her and sat on the edge of the
bed, his breaths coming in harsh pants as he covered
his face with his hands.

"Travis?" She sat up next to him, a hand on his arm.

He moved his hands down from his face, his eyes
filled with deep regret. "Elena..." Gently his fingers
moved to the front of her nightgown, where they
worked to refasten the buttons. "Elena...it's not
right...I can't make love to you. Not yet."

He finished with the last button, then placed his hands
on either side of her face. "Elena. You have to remember, right now it feels as if I've only known you a week.
And while I've grown to care for you in that time, it's
too soon for lovemaking." He leaned forward and
pressed his lips against her forehead. "I can't make love
to a woman I can't remember loving. I'm sorry." He
dropped his hands and looked away, as if afraid of her
anger.

"Travis, don't apologize." She traced a finger down
the side of his jawline. "I pushed too fast. You're right,
it's much too soon." Although disappointed, Elena was
also touched by his words. And the fact that he didn't
want to make love to a woman he couldn't remember
loving, only made her love him more.

She stood, her hand lingering against the warmth of

his cheek. "Good night, Travis," she whispered, then left his room.

Once again in her room, she slid back beneath the bed covers. Although his words had made her love him more than ever, they hadn't assuaged the deep hunger that still coursed through her.

She lay on her back, staring up at the ceiling where the moonlight danced and played like an impish spirit. The Travis she had known before the accident wouldn't have hesitated making love to any woman. Love or the absence of, wouldn't have hindered him in reaching for personal pleasure.

She closed her eyes, trying to ignore the wish that suddenly tried to form inside her head, deep in her heart. But despite her resolve to the contrary, the wish grew stronger and stronger until she couldn't ignore it, she could only accept that what she wanted more than anything, was for Travis's memories to remain lost forever.

He waited nearly an hour before he finally crept out of bed and yanked on his jeans. He needed to get fresh air, get out of this house that smelled of her, breathed with her essence.

Like a thief in the night, Trent made his way out of his room, through the kitchen and out the back door without making a sound.

He drew deep breaths of the cool night air, trying to rid himself of the smell of her, the taste of her, the very feel of her warm skin against his. Heaven help him, but he'd wanted her. He'd wanted to go on touching her, kissing her, loving her until they were both sated and spent.

As he walked across the small back porch, the bare

wood creaked and groaned. The dewy grass was cool beneath his feet as he left the porch and headed for the corral, needing to walk off the lingering desire that ached in his body.

He walked around the corral, the silence of the night pressing in on him. There should be sound…the lowing of cattle from a nearby pasture, the snorts and pawing of horses in the corral. But of course it was difficult to have livestock if there wasn't any money. And Elena's money had been stolen…embezzled by a woman with short blond hair named Lydia. A woman who had written a note to Travis calling him a double-crossing snake.

The desire that had soared through him transformed to a soul sickness that nearly stole his breath. Trent knew. He knew with certainty that his brother had transpired with Lydia Walsh to steal Elena's and Cameron's trust funds. Somehow, someway, he had to find Travis, and he had a feeling if he was patient, Lydia Walsh might give him the clues that would point to Travis's whereabouts.

Patience. He drew in a deep gulp of air, once again remembering those moments of holding Elena in his arms, of tasting her sweet skin, caressing her heated flesh. As much as he'd wanted to take her, to make love to her, he hadn't been able to follow through on that desire. Because it was wrong. Because it was a lie. But mostly because if he ever did make love to her, it was his name he wanted her to sigh in the throes of passion. His name…not his brother's.

Chapter 7

It was early Monday morning when Cameron called to say he was bringing Elena's horses over. Trent immediately went out to fill the tank in the corral with water and shovel fresh hay into the barn stalls where the horses would be kept at night.

As he used a pitchfork to arrange the sweet-smelling hay, his thoughts were far away from the task at hand. Tonight was when he was supposed to meet the short-haired blond woman at the usual place.

The usual place.

Where in the hell was the usual place?

He paused a moment, leaning on the handle...and tried to think like his brother. But it was useless. The ways of Travis's mind had always been foreign territory to Trent. There was a mean, almost evil streak in Travis that Trent had never understood.

Both men had been raised with the same loving parents, in a stable, secure environment. Both had shared the privileges of upper middle-class life, and yet Travis had chosen wrong paths from the time he was very young. He'd thought nothing of stealing and seemed to find lying easier than telling the truth.

For a long time it had worried Trent. After all, they came not only from the same background, but from the same egg...identical in genetic makeup.

Did Trent carry a piece of that evil inside him? Is that what made him desire his brother's wife? Was there a strand of immoral thread running through him as well as through his brother?

He muttered an irritable curse as he continued placing hay in the second stall. As he worked, a vision of Elena drifted through his head...a picture of how she had looked the night of the dance when she'd come to his room.

She'd been clad in a white nightgown that glowed almost incandescently in the silvery moonlight. She'd smelled of summer nights and mystery, and when she'd moved into his arms, he'd felt as if the world had momentarily tilted and nothing would ever be quite the same again.

Although he'd managed to call a halt to their lovemaking, it had taken every ounce of self control he possessed. Even now, replaying those moments of having her in his arms, tasting the sweetness of her lips, his knees weakened with want and his pulse pounded with an erratic rhythm.

If she came to him again, needy and wanting, he wasn't sure he'd have the resources to turn down what she offered. He wanted to believe he could, because accepting the gift of her lovemaking would be wrong. He'd be accepting under false pretenses.

He'd just finished in the stables when he heard the rumble of horses approaching. He stepped out of the barn to see Cameron arriving. He rode his big black horse and two slightly smaller, golden palominos trailed behind him.

Trent stepped out to greet him, watching as he dismounted. Cameron opened the corral gate and led the two horses into the enclosure. He took off their bridles, then offered them each something out of his pocket. Giving each a final pat on the rump, he stepped out of the corral and shut the gate.

"Nice-looking horses," Trent observed as he watched the two exploring their new home, silvery tails blowing in the gentle breeze.

"Elena has a good eye. When she bought them, they were too thin and more than a little wild, but she saw their potential. All they needed was a gentle hand and a good, steady diet."

It was the most words Cameron had ever said to him. "Elena said you were good with horses."

Cameron shrugged. "They seem to trust me. I like horses. It's people I have problems with."

Elena rushed out the back door, hair flying behind here as she raced toward them, face shining with excitement. "Oh, Cam, they look wonderful," she exclaimed. "I knew they'd be beautiful after a few weeks in your care."

Like a child, she climbed up on the bottom rung of the corral and held out a hand, beckoning the horses toward her. They pranced around the pen, as if showing off their beauty, but didn't approach her until Cameron handed her several pieces of apple.

It was finally the larger of the two that whinnied a greeting and was bold enough to take the apple from her palm. Within seconds, both stood near her, allowing her to stroke their necks and muzzles.

Trent watched her as she sweet-talked the horses, a flutter of desire beginning in the pit of his stomach. She looked so beautiful, with the sun shining on her dark hair and happiness radiating from within, reflecting on her features.

Ever since Friday night, when he'd nearly lost his soul by making love to her, desire had struck him at odd moments each and every day. Every single act she performed, even simply walking across the room, made Trent's blood boil with desire, his stomach ache with unfulfillment. And she seemed to have no idea of her effect on him.

With her attention occupied on the horses, Trent moved closer to Cameron. "So, you were a bounty hunter before you became a rancher."

"That's right."

"Elena told me you came out of retirement to look for Lydia Walsh. Cold trail?"

A dark shadow crossed Cameron's features. "No trail. One day she was in her office in Billings. The next day she was gone."

"Does she have family? Parents?"

Cameron nodded. "Her mother and father live in Billings, but they haven't heard from her. From what little I was able to glean, there had been a rift in that relationship and at the time she disappeared, it had been months since she'd spoken with her family. She has a sister in the area, but the sister insists she hasn't seen or heard from Lydia in months.'' He eyed Trent suspiciously. ''Why the sudden interest?''

''Just curious.'' Trent looked back at Elena. ''Lydia Walsh stole a fortune from somebody I care about. It would be nice if she was found and the money was returned. Then Elena could build the kind of ranch she's always dreamed of owning here.''

''That's rich…coming from you. You never seemed too interested before in seeing Elena's dreams come true.''

''I want her to be happy…and secure,'' Trent said succinctly.

Cameron stared at him for another long moment, then mounted his horse. ''I've got to get back to my place. Those horses need to be exercised daily. Obviously Elena can't ride right now, so it will be up to you to see to them.''

Trent nodded. He'd grown up on a ranch in Southern California. Even though it had been years since he'd ridden, he knew it was a skill rarely lost forever. ''I can handle it.''

Saying goodbye to his sister, Cameron then rode away. As the sound of his horse hooves faded, Trent joined Elena at the corral. She turned to him, eyes shining. ''Oh, Travis, it's so exciting. This is just the beginning. Eventually I want a dozen horses.''

He grinned at her enthusiasm. ''Might be a little difficult for these two to be the beginning of more, being that both of them are mares.''

She laughed. ''I know. I need a stallion. I've been keeping my eye out for the perfect breeder. I'll know him when I see him." Her smile deepened and her hand went to her stomach.

He felt himself drowning in the sweet emotion that radiated from her eyes. His chest hurt as if he were suffocating, swallowing water instead of air. He flailed to the surface and tore his gaze from hers. "I should be able to finish painting the barn today." When he looked back at her, the emotion that had drawn him under was gone.

"That will be nice." She gazed once again at the horses. "Travis, what happens when you never get your memory back?"

He knew what she was really asking. What would happen between them? Would they ever make love again? Did they have a future together if he never got his memories back. He paused a moment before answering. "Eventually it will all come back to me," he said, knowing he hadn't answered her question, but he had no real answer.

Tell her, an inner voice shouted. Tell her the truth now. Trent opened his mouth to follow the inner voice's advice, then snapped it shut once again.

Tonight was the night he would hopefully meet the woman who had sent him the strange note. He didn't want to jeopardize things by coming clean to Elena...at least not yet.

"I'd better get busy." Without looking at her again, he strode off toward the barn.

Elena watched him go, as always a myriad of emotions swirling inside her. If he never got his memories back, would they be able to build a life together, a life filled with love, with desire...with joy and laughter? Without his memories would he eventually be able to make love to her? Or would he keep himself distant, as he'd done since the night of the dance, unwilling to enjoy physical intimacy with a woman he didn't remember?

She turned and went back into the house, wishing Travis's return hadn't brought with it such chaos to her thoughts. If he'd come back the same man who had disappeared, she'd have had no problem in divorcing him, cutting him out of her life forever.

Unfortunately that wasn't the case. He'd come back possessing all the character traits Elena had wished for, tunneling his way into her heart despite her natural caution.

She jumped as the phone rang. She hurried into the kitchen and grabbed the receiver from the wall phone. "Hello?"

Silence...although Elena could hear the whisper of a breath, knew somebody was on the other end of the line.

"Hello? Is somebody there?"

There was another moment of silence, then the click of the connection being broken.

Thoughtfully, Elena hung up the receiver. She'd forgotten about the calls. Calls that had jingled the phone all hours of the day and night in the month before Travis had disappeared.

She poured herself a glass of iced tea, then sank into a chair at the table. The calls had started almost immediately after their wedding. The phone would ring, Elena would answer, and whoever was on the other end would hang up. The hang-ups never came when Travis was home. When he answered the phone there was always somebody on the other end of the line.

Elena had begun to suspect that perhaps Travis was

having an affair. But when she'd asked him about it, he'd protested his innocence and she'd believed him because she so wanted to believe him.

"You ninny," she berated herself aloud. "It was just one phone call." Probably on a single day in the town of Mustang a dozen people got hang-up calls.

The baby stirred, fluttering against her stomach as if eager to be free. Elena placed a hand over her tummy and rubbed softly.

She'd meant to talk to Travis about the spare room. They needed to transform the little room into a nursery. With only four months of pregnancy left, it was time to start preparing for the arrival of their son or daughter.

Instantly her head filled with a vision of a rich wooden crib and matching dressing table...frills and bows and the scent of baby powder. It would be such fun decorating the room for the baby.

She'd also meant to ask him about attending Lamaze classes with her. She wanted a natural birth, with Travis there to aid in the delivery.

She closed her eyes, able to imagine that glorious moment. Travis would hold her hand, stroke her brow, encouraging her with love shining bright in his eyes. And when the baby finally entered the world, they would be a family and their love would see them through any difficult times ahead.

A shiver of happiness danced up her spine at the beautiful vision. It could happen, she told herself. It's possible we can have a happy ending.

The forced sex on the ridge so long ago, his emotional stinginess seemed distant...too distant to mar her hopes for the future. She rubbed her stomach and smiled softly. She'd ask him about setting up a nursery and attending Lamaze classes with her at dinner.

"Don't tell me you're one of those hopeless romantics who believes love conquers all."

Travis's words from the night of the dance came back to her. She'd told him she used to believe that…but wasn't sure what she believed anymore. She'd lied. She was still a hopeless romantic.

When she'd married Travis, she'd wanted a marriage like her parents had enjoyed, a relationship built not only on love and desire, but also mutual respect and shared hopes and dreams.

In the month of marriage to Travis, those dreams had flickered out, squashed beneath his sneering derision and casual cruelty. She'd fought with herself every day, wanting out of the marriage, but reluctant to give up on those dreams.

She rose from the table and went to the back window. Staring out toward the barn in the distance, she could see Travis on a ladder, finishing the last of the painting.

Maybe he will remain the same even when he gets his memory back, she thought hopefully. Maybe fate had somehow given them a second chance to make those wonderful dreams come true.

Only time would tell if she was being given a second chance for happiness. Or if this was just another opportunity for fate to kick her in the face.

"Travis?"

He looked at her as he spooned mashed potatoes onto his plate. "Yes?"

"I was wondering if maybe in the next week or two

we could go into town and pick up a few things for the spare room?"

"The spare room?" He set down the bowl of potatoes. "You mean the one I'm in?"

She shook her head. "No, the smallest one at the end of the hall. It will be the baby's room. But we need to buy a crib and a changing table and start stocking the nursery with the things the baby will need."

Once again that suffocating feeling came over Trent. The feeling that he was in too deep, drowning in Travis's life. "Uh...sure. We can get whatever you need."

He jumped as she reached across the table and covered his hand with hers. "I have another favor to ask you."

"What's that?" He tried not to focus on the warmth of her hand. He didn't want to think about how her hands had stroked down his bare back, evoking licks of fire as she'd urged him to make love to her.

"When the baby is born...I want you there with me...in the delivery room."

Trent felt the blood drain from his face. All too easily he could imagine being there...being an integral part of the miracle of birth. But, like a cactus growing in a Montana pasture, he didn't belong in the vision. "Oh, Elena...I don't know."

She tightened her hand on his and smiled. "Come on, Travis. You've never struck me as the squeamish type before. This is so important. I know you won't be sorry. I want you there with me the moment our baby comes into the world."

"Okay," he answered, knowing he'd be gone from her life long before the birth.

"Terrific," she exclaimed and to his relief, removed her hand from his.

Terrific, he mentally echoed with more than a touch of anger directed at himself. He was building hope, promising a future that would never exist and guilt made his appetite flee.

The evening hours crept by. Elena turned on the television and they watched several shows. Between programs and during the commercials, she talked about the things she wanted to get accomplished around the ranch before winter set in.

"Elena, what are you living on? I mean, your trust fund was stolen. You don't have a job, and I've certainly been no financial help. How are you existing?" he asked curiously.

She shrugged and tucked her feet up beneath her on the sofa. "I told you I was a teacher before moving here to Mustang. I taught for three years, lived in a tiny apartment and saved whatever money I could. I had quite a little nest egg when my parents died, and I bought this place. I've still got some of that money left and in the last couple of months I've rented out some of my pasture to neighbors."

"What happens when your nest egg is gone?" he asked.

She frowned and twirled a strand of her dark hair around a finger. "I'm not sure. Initially, I'd hoped to have the ranch up and running, financially working itself by that time. I figured the trust fund would help me accomplish that." She shrugged. "I'm just taking things one day at a time right now. Hopefully the future will take care of itself."

Soon after their conversation, she excused herself and

went to bed. Trent was glad to see her go and hoped she would sleep deeply, so soundly she wouldn't hear him later when he left for the Roundup.

He shut off the television, walked through the kitchen and stepped out the back door. Night had fallen, but the moon overhead illuminated the land in a pale silvery glow.

Elena had chosen well. Although the house and other buildings needed work, the surrounding fields and pastures were lush with rich dark soil and tall green grass.

As he stepped off the back porch and approached the corral, the horses nickered greetings, dancing toward the gate as if anticipating a night ride.

"Sorry girls, not tonight," he said softly. Leaning against the corral, he allowed the serene songs of the night to sweep through him. Crickets chirped, the horses pawed and snorted, and a light breeze rustled through the leaves of a stand of trees nearby.

Peaceful. It reminded him of his childhood, growing up on a southern California ranch. His parents had owned the ranch until Trent and Travis were fifteen, then they sold out and moved to the city. It had been Trent's dream to one day live again on a ranch just like this.

Funny, that it had been Trent's dream, and yet Travis had been the one to achieve that dream. Travis had a wife, a ranch with endless possibilities, and had thrown it all away. If what Trent suspected was true, Travis had traded this place and Elena for a satchel full of money. As he stood, breathing in the sweet scent of the ranch, his mind filled with visions of Elena, Trent knew his brother had chosen the short end of the stick.

He moved back to the porch and sank down in a

chair, thinking of the requests Elena had made over dinner. Stocking a nursery...being in the delivery room when the baby is born...things that should be between a husband and wife...the kind of things that nurtured love and commitment.

He could help her pick out items for the nursery, but he'd be long gone before it came time for her to deliver the baby. He didn't belong here. This game of pretense was just that...a game to flush out the truth about his brother.

He remained outside until it was eleven-thirty, then he got into the car and headed for the Roundup. As he drove, he kept his mind studiously focused away from Elena and toward the meeting he anticipated.

It was just a guess...that the back room of the Roundup was the usual meeting place for Travis and Lydia Walsh. He hoped it was the correct guess, because he needed to get out of his present situation.

He had to escape from the bewitchment of Elena.

He had to leave before it was too late.... Before he was not only guilty of coveting his brother's wife...but of possessing her as well.

Chapter 8

Despite it being a Monday night, the Roundup was jumping when Trent entered the noisy, smoky saloon. He made his way to the bar and signaled to Sam.

"The usual?" Sam asked.

Trent shook his head. "A beer and maybe a little information?"

Sam's dark eyebrows raised in curiosity. He drew a beer from the tap, then set it down before Trent. "What kind of information?"

"When I was meeting that blond woman here, how was it arranged? I mean, did I wait out here until she showed up, then we went to your back room or what?"

Sam grinned knowingly. "You sly devil. You meeting her again?"

Trent nodded curtly, slightly sickened by Sam's easy acceptance of what he assumed was Travis's infidelity.

"I'm supposed to meet her tonight at midnight. I just don't remember how we did it in the past."

"That amnesia thing, right?"

"Yeah, something like that." Trent took a drink of his beer, wishing it could take away the bad taste in his mouth.

"Does Elena know you're here?"

Trent eyed him wryly. "What do you think?"

Sam laughed. "Okay, this is how it always went down. You went to the back room and waited for the blonde. She'd knock on the back door and you'd let her in. She never came through the bar, she always arrived and left by the back door."

"You mind if I go back and see if she shows?"

"No, Travis. You know I don't mind." Sam gestured to the narrow doorway behind the bar. "You can go on back whenever you want."

"Thanks, Sam. And this is our little secret?" Trent forced himself to wink suggestively.

Sam grinned. "No problem, Travis. Mum's the word."

With a nod to Sam, Trent rounded the end of the bar and walked through the doorway that led to the back area of the establishment. He found himself in a small storage room.

A desk was shoved up against one wall, the top nearly covered with invoices and miscellaneous paperwork. Metal shelving rose from floor to ceiling against the other walls, holding napkins, glassware, booze and mixers and a variety of other items used to keep the Roundup running smoothly. Two folding chairs were propped against one of the shelves.

Trent opened the back door, discovered it led into a

small dark alley. He closed it once again, making certain it remained unlocked. He checked his watch. Eleven-forty-five. He grabbed one of the folding chairs, opened it and sat, trying to still the racing beat of his heart.

Hopefully, in fifteen or twenty minutes he would know what had happened to his brother. He would know if Travis was responsible for Elena's and Cam's missing trust funds. He would know if his worst suspicions about his brother were true.

If his suspicions were true, then Travis had irrevocably lost his soul to the evil of avarice. Trent had always hoped that eventually his brother would find happiness. He'd hoped that eventually Travis would settle down to a normal life, find a woman whose love would be enough to make him happy, fulfilled. Trent had always prayed that eventually Travis would be redeemed, but if what he suspected was true, it was too late for redemption.

Trent looked at his watch once again. Eleven-fifty-five. Five more minutes and Lydia Walsh might walk through the door. The second hand on his watch crept round and round, ticking off the minutes in an agonizingly slow march of time.

Midnight came and went. He tried to convince himself she was just late, that eventually she'd arrive and with her the answers he sought. But by quarter after twelve, his stomach was in knots as he realized it was possible he'd guessed wrong. Maybe the Roundup wasn't their usual meeting place.

He left the Roundup just before one, knowing she wasn't going to show. Either he was at the wrong place or for some reason Lydia had changed her mind about meeting with him.

As he drove back to Elena's, he wondered what would happen next. How would Lydia contact him? There was no doubt in his mind that she would. After all, the note she'd sent him implied a double cross, and the fact that Travis had her share of the money.

He sneaked back into the house and into bed, frustration keeping sleep at bay for most of the night. It was near dawn when he finally fell into a restless sleep disturbed by nightmares.

He awoke to the sound of ringing. The phone. He cracked an eyelid and looked at the clock on the bedside table. Almost eight. He'd slept much later than usual. Tossing the sheet back, he swung his legs over the side of the bed, frowning as the phone continued its demand for attention.

Where was Elena? He grabbed his jeans and yanked them on, then stumbled out of the bedroom. Elena wasn't in the living room, nor was she in the kitchen. He grabbed up the phone receiver and breathed a hello at the same time he spied Elena out at the corral visiting the horses.

"Where were you last night? I'll teach you to jerk me around. Give me my half of the money or your sweet little wife might get hurt."

Before Trent could utter a single word, the buzz of a dial tone told him the caller had hung up. "Damn." He slammed the receiver down, fighting against a chill that threatened to crawl up his spine.

She hadn't given him a chance to explain that he didn't know where she wanted him to meet her. She hadn't given him a chance to say anything.

He raked a hand through his hair, then poured himself a cup of coffee. Moving to the window, he sipped the brew and watched Elena petting the horses.

Clad in a yellow shift, she looked like a dollop of sunshine amid the greens and earth tones of the surrounding landscape. Her hair was caught at the nape of her neck with a wide barrette, creating a waterfall of darkness that reached nearly to the middle of her back.

The case of Travis's disappearance had suddenly taken an appalling turn. The caller had threatened Elena if she didn't receive her half of the money. And Trent had no idea where his brother might be, although it was certain that wherever Travis was...the money was with him.

Trent finished his coffee and poured himself another cup, knowing he was avoiding the fact that he had to tell Elena the truth. If the threat toward her was real, then she had a right to know about it. And there was no reason to believe that Lydia Walsh wasn't the kind of woman who was capable of following through on a threat.

Elena would hate him when he told her he wasn't Travis. And he couldn't blame her. She would hate him for pretending, for building hope inside her that they could be a happy family.

Regret surged up inside him. It had been a foolish idea, for him to pretend to be his brother. Travis's betrayal would be difficult enough for her to accept, but by borrowing Travis's identity, Trent had only made things worse for her.

He heard the sharp report of a gunshot and almost instantaneously the dirt next to Elena's feet seemed to explode. The horses reared up, their frightened screams filling the air. Elena appeared to freeze, her eyes widened in alarm.

It took only a moment for Trent to realize what had happened. He dropped his coffee cup, barely conscious of it shattering as it hit the floor. Heart pounding, he raced out the back door. He jumped off the porch as another shot cracked in the air. "Elena, get down!" he yelled as he dived toward her.

The initial paralysis that had frozen her snapped and she ran and crouched down behind the galvanized water tank. Trent joined her there, an arm around her protectively. "You all right?"

"I…I guess. Travis, what's happening?"

He felt the trembling of her body against his, cursed himself for not taking immediate action following the threatening phone call. "I'll explain everything later," he said, his gaze focused on the stand of trees where the shots seemed to have originated.

They remained behind the trough…not moving, not talking…for long minutes. Trent kept his attention solely on the copse of trees, looking for movement, a flash of clothing, anything that would tell him where the shooter was hidden.

Nothing. He saw nothing, heard nothing. The horses remained skittish. They danced nervously around the corral and kicked up clouds of dust. He heard the pounding of a heart, and wasn't sure if it was Elena's or his own.

His arm tightened around her, sheer horror sweeping through him as he thought of how close those bullets had come. An inch, that's all they had missed her by. A frighteningly small inch.

More minutes passed. Minutes of pounding hearts,

fear-laced breaths and intense vigilance. Trent's muscles burned from the unnatural crouch he was in, and he knew Elena's were probably burning as well. But she said nothing.

Trent waited another minute or two, then cautiously rose up, anticipating the possibility of another shot. Nothing. He stood straight, facing the trees where he knew the shooter had been. Still nothing.

Was she hiding there in the trees with his body in her crosshairs? Or was she waiting for Elena to stand, then she'd pull the trigger.

Of course it was possible the shots had been a warning and now that the warning had been given, Lydia Walsh had once again crawled back beneath whatever rock she'd been hiding under.

"Elena, I want you to stand up and get right behind me," he instructed. If Lydia was there, he realized with a certainty she wouldn't shoot him. She thought he had her money. She wouldn't risk killing him without getting what she believed he owed her.

Elena stood, her body pressed tightly against his back. "Now, we're going to walk to the house, but I want you to keep my body between you and those trees," he instructed.

"But Travis..."

"Just do what I say," he snapped, interrupting her protest.

Together they made their way toward the porch, Trent shielding her with his body. Step by step, they moved slowly...cautiously.

No gunshot rang out and Trent noted that the horses had settled down, as if sensing the danger had passed.

Still, he didn't breath a sigh of relief until they were safely inside the house.

"Are you sure you're all right?" he asked worriedly as Elena sank down on the sofa. The bottom of her dress was dust covered and her features were taut with strain.

"I'm fine considering somebody just tried to kill me." Her lower lip quivered and she wrapped her arms around her shoulders, as if to stave off a chill. She drew a tremulous breath and stared up at him. "Travis, will you please tell me what's going on?"

He frowned, knowing he had no other choice. It was time for him to tell her the truth. It was time for him to break her heart. "Elena, my name isn't Travis. It's Trent. I'm not your husband, I'm your husband's twin brother."

Elena stared at him, struggling to make sense of his words. "Is this some kind of a sick joke?" she finally managed to ask. That was it, it had to be a joke. He'd thought it was funny to scare her on the ridge that morning long ago. This was more of his perverse sense of humor. "Travis, this isn't even remotely funny."

He sat down next to her on the sofa, his expression remorseful. "It's no joke. I know this is confusing for you."

"Confusing?" She bit back a hysterical burst of laughter, her gaze studying his features intently. She raised a hand, as if to touch his face, trace the line of his jaw. "You're lying. Why are you doing this to me?"

"I'm sorry, Elena. It's the truth."

The face that she stared at belonged to her husband, belonged to Travis. Instead of touching his face, she clenched her hands together in her lap, unsure what to believe. "You…you look just like him. How do I know you aren't him?"

"What reason would I have to lie?" His face reddened slightly. "I mean, I lied before, when I said I was Travis, but that was because I've been trying to find out what happened to him." He stood and reached into his back pocket and withdrew a wallet. Flipping it open, he showed her his driver's license, complete with his photo and the name Trent Richards.

Elena's world crumbled around her, leaving her bewildered, afraid…and more than a little angry. She stood, found her legs trembling and weak and sat down once again. "I don't understand. If you're Trent…then where is Travis?" She frowned, trying to ignore her anger, avoid her fear.

"That's what I came here to find out."

She stared at him in wonder. A twin…an identical twin. "He never told me about you. He said he had no family, that his parents were dead and he was an only child. Never did he mention you."

Trent's features tightened. "Travis spent most of his life denying my existence. I'm not surprised that's what he told you."

"But…why would he lie? Why would he lie to me?" Her voice quivered uncontrollably and she felt the hot press of tears burning her eyes. "I was…I am his wife."

She stood, her legs no longer shaking, but strong and firm as anger coursed through her. "How dare you," she said, her outrage vibrant in her voice. "How dare you stay in my home, eat my food, and…and everything while pretending to be him."

Her face flushed hot as she thought of the night of

the dance, when she'd gone into his bedroom. She'd kissed him…and he'd kissed her back. She'd caressed him…and he'd returned each of her touches with heated ones of his own. She'd believed he was her husband. But he had no such excuse for his behavior.

"Look, I know what I did was wrong." His gaze didn't meet hers. Instead he stared at some indefinable point just above her left shoulder. "I didn't think it through, didn't consider the consequences." His gaze finally met hers, and in his eyes she saw his regret and her anger seeped away.

She sank back down on the sofa, and succumbed to the confusion that swirled inside her head. "So if you aren't Travis, then is…is Travis…dead?" The word came with difficulty. "Did he fall off the ridge that day?"

"I don't think so." He sat down next to her on the sofa. "I'm fairly certain he walked off that ridge, somehow he got down without you seeing him."

She stared at him for a long moment, trying to make sense of his words. "But why? Why would he do something like that?"

"For money," he answered flatly.

"For money?" she echoed him without understanding. Then realization struck and with it a heaviness that crashed into her heart. "My trust fund?"

He nodded, pain darkening his eyes to a midnight blue. "I think Travis conspired with Lydia Walsh to steal the trust funds."

"I don't believe you." Tears once again threatened to fall. If what he said was true, everything she'd believed in was destroyed. Even though she had thought she probably would divorce Travis, Trent's supposition made a mockery of the entire marriage. Angrily she swiped at her eyes, refusing to allow this man...this stranger to see her cry. "So, who shot at us and why? Travis?"

"No. I think it was Lydia. I think somehow Travis double-crossed her. Apparently Travis didn't tell her about me, either. She thinks I'm Travis and she wants her half of the money."

Elena rubbed her forehead, confusion again battling with heartache. She hadn't realized until this moment how much hope she'd harbored. Her dreams of a happy marriage to Travis had seemed a distinct possibility in the last week. She looked at Trent, almost hating him for his pretense that had given her hope, then snatching it away in a matter of minutes.

"Elena, I'm so sorry," he said as if reading her mind. He reached out a hand and touched her arm in a gesture meant to be soothing.

She pulled away from his touch. "How do you know all this? Why are you here? What part are you planning in this supposed scheme?"

"I work as a private investigator in California. Over a week ago my secretary brought me a missing persons flyer. It had a picture of Travis on it. That was the first I knew about him disappearing. Knowing Travis the way I do, I decided to come out and snoop around, see what I could find out."

He stood, as if unable to gather his thoughts without pacing the floor in front of her. "I suspected perhaps you and Travis were trying to scam the insurance company for money. But the moment I walked through your garden gate, I knew you had nothing to do with any of this scheme."

He paused...frowned, then continued. "It was also in that moment that I decided to step into Travis's shoes, see if perhaps by living his life I could figure out exactly what had happened to him."

He stopped pacing and dug into his back pocket. He withdrew a note and handed it to her. "I was given that on the night of the dance."

Elena read the note and the last of her doubts concerning Travis's innocence fell away, leaving a deep ache of hurt as she realized he'd probably married her for a single reason...her trust fund.

"We need to go to the sheriff," she finally said as she set the note on the coffee table. "Apparently Lydia is in the area. We'd all assumed she'd flown off to some exotic location to spend my money. The sheriff needs to know she's somewhere close by so he can find her and arrest her."

"No. We can't go to the sheriff. Not yet," he protested. Again he sat down next to her on the sofa. "Lydia thinks I'm Travis, and as long as she believes that, she'll continue to contact me for her share of the money. But if we go to the sheriff, he might tell somebody, and somebody else will tell another person and within hours the whole town of Mustang will know I'm not Travis."

"So what do we do?"

"We wait. We keep pretending I'm your husband. Apparently Lydia hasn't heard about my supposed amnesia. When she contacts me again, I'll tell her about it and make her tell me the details of what she and Travis did and planned."

"If what you think is true, Lydia just tried to shoot

us. You really think she's going to have a calm, rational conversation with you?'' Elena asked dryly.

"I don't think she was shooting at me, and I don't think she intended to hurt you. She called earlier and said that if I didn't give her the money, you might get hurt.''

"Thanks for sharing that after the fact," Elena said bitterly. She felt as if she'd entered a nightmare and no matter how she tried, she couldn't wake up.

"I think those shots were a warning. She wants Travis to know she means business."

"You keep talking about Lydia...what about Travis? Where is he?''

He frowned. "I don't know. But I think eventually I'll hear from him. Travis has always been a braggart. If he pulled off such an enormous scam, he'll need to brag to somebody, and I've always been his victim in that regard.''

Elena studied him curiously, still finding it so amazing how identical he was to Travis. And yet not identical, she reminded herself, thinking of the positive traits he'd displayed for the last week. "You don't like your brother very much, do you?''

"I love my brother," he replied emphatically. "He's a part of my heart, a part of my soul. When I read he was presumed dead, I knew it wasn't true. If Travis was dead, I'd feel it...here." He touched his chest, then sighed. "I love him, but I've never understood him. I don't like the choices he's made in his life.''

Elena sighed wearily. It was all so confusing...so heartbreaking. She thought of telling Trent that she'd intended to leave his brother, that Travis hadn't been the man she'd thought him to be. But what was the point? He knew his brother's negative traits and in any case, none of it mattered anymore.

"So I'm back in limbo," she finally said. "I'm married to a man who has disappeared and nobody knows where to find him." The baby turned and bumped and she pressed a hand lightly against her stomach, tears blurring her vision.

She stood, not wanting to cry in front of Trent, yet needing to weep for all that was lost. "If you'll excuse me, I think I need to lie down." She ran for her bedroom before he could see the tears that streaked down her cheeks.

In the privacy of her room, she let the tears flow. Even though she'd intended to divorce Travis before his disappearance, his profound betrayal sent waves of pain crashing into the chambers of her heart.

If what Trent suspected was true, then Travis had never loved her. At their ceremony when he'd gazed into her eyes, he hadn't seen her love…he'd seen dollar signs.

She'd been such a fool. Despite his unexplained absences, in spite of his secrecy and lies, she'd been willing to try to make it work, had loved him enough to overlook so many things.

And in the last week with Trent, she'd once again been willing to overlook the past and build a new future with Travis. God, she'd been a fool, believing that somehow Travis's personality had been enriched with empathy and gentleness from a bump on his head.

She sobbed out her pain, her anguish, muffling her cries with her pillow. She ached with her loss. The loss of a husband…the loss of a father for her child. If

Travis had stolen her money, he certainly wasn't the kind of a man she'd want to parent her child.

Damn Trent Richards for his game of switched identities. Travis might have stolen her money, but Trent had done something almost as bad. He'd given her back her hope for a future filled with love, then destroyed it once again. In the last week, she'd grown to care for him.

How utterly ludicrous, that she'd believed she was once again falling in love with her husband...but instead she'd been falling in love with her husband's brother. Damn him for betraying her by giving her false hope about her marriage, about her future. He'd made her love him, and for that she'd never forgive him.

He had to leave. She didn't want him here. He had the face of the man she'd married, and the character of the man she could love. But he wasn't her husband, and having to pretend he was played havoc with her emotions.

And yet...she sat up, tears spent. If it was just her money that had been stolen, she would have told Trent to forget the whole thing and go back where he came from. But it wasn't just her money. Cameron's money had been embezzled as well, and Elena wanted justice. She wanted Lydia Walsh behind bars. And if Travis was part of that conspiracy, then he belonged behind bars as well.

Trent was right in that if Lydia was to be caught, the best course of action appeared to be to continue the deception.

She would have to pretend that Trent was Travis.

She would have to pretend that Trent was her loving husband come back to her.

Wiping the remnants of her tears from her face, she got up off the bed. Fine. She would continue the game in order to catch the thieves. But there had to be rules.

She went back into the living room, where Trent stood staring out the picture window. He must have heard her enter the room, for he turned around to face her.

"Two weeks," she said without preamble. "For the next two weeks I'll pretend that you're Travis. But if nothing happens in that time, I'm going to the sheriff with everything we know."

He nodded, his features revealing nothing of his thoughts. "You realize you might be in danger from Lydia. While I believe the shots today were merely a warning, there's no guarantee what she might do next."

Elena's heart quivered as fear rippled up her spine. "I realize that. However I don't intend to give Lydia another chance to shoot at me. For the next two weeks I don't intend on leaving this house."

Anger surged up, momentarily replacing her fear. "No matter what happens, at the end of those two weeks, I want you out of here. I've had enough of the Richards men to last a lifetime." With these words she turned and went back to her bedroom.

Chapter 9

Trent had known she would be angry. As he'd begun his confession he'd seen the disbelief in her eyes slowly transform to flames of fury. Her anger had been easy to accept. He deserved it.

Nor was he surprised by the fact that she wanted him out of her house, out of her life. What did surprise him was that she was willing to give him two weeks to continue his pretense.

When she'd come out of her bedroom to give him that ultimatum, her eyes had been red and swollen, testimony to the fact that her anger had passed and she'd plunged right into heartache. He'd broken her heart with his deception. First Travis, then himself.

He paced the living room, angry with himself for his choice in becoming involved in Travis's life. When his secretary had brought him the flyer announcing Travis's disappearance, Trent should have filed it in the trash can and forgotten it.

Things would have been much less complicated if he had written Travis out of his life a long time ago. But...how did one go about writing off a brother? Especially a twin?

In the last days of his mother's illness, it had been her wish that her sons would make peace with one another. She'd known Travis's faults, had loved him in spite of them and had encouraged Trent to do the same. Find forgiveness, she'd begged him.

He left the living room and walked into the kitchen, not wanting to think of his mother and her last wish. At the window he stared out past the corral, to the copse of trees where he guessed Lydia had been when she'd shot at them.

How had she found the time to call him, then get positioned in those trees so quickly? There had only been a few minutes between the phone call and the shots. The answer came to him instantly. A cellular phone.

She'd watched Elena out at the corral, and had called the house, knowing Trent was alone inside and would answer the phone. Apparently she was still playing the game of subterfuge, believing that Travis wouldn't...couldn't tell Elena what was going on.

Trent narrowed his eyes in thought. She could be watching the house right now...waiting for the next opportunity to contact him.

Unsure whether it was smart or not, Trent opened the back door and stepped outside. Part of his success as a private investigator came with his talent for getting into the mind of his prey.

This time was different. He didn't know enough about Lydia to anticipate her moves, ferret out her hiding places. He couldn't begin to guess what she might do next...and that worried him.

He stepped off the porch and began walking. The midmorning sun was pleasantly warm on his shoulders as he moved briskly through the grass. As he strode past the corral the horses nickered a greeting, but Trent didn't stop. He kept his gaze focused on the group of trees, his steady gait bringing him closer and closer.

He remained tense, ready to jump and dive, bob and weave should a bullet come his way. But he felt no sense of impeding doom. Birds sang from the trees and somewhere nearby a squirrel chattered angrily as Trent entered the cool shadows and thick underbrush. He knew with certainty that Lydia might have been here earlier, but she wasn't hiding here now.

He walked from tree to tree, studying the ground, seeking the place where she'd stood or crouched in order to fire a gun at them.

He found the spot at the base of a huge gnarled tree. The tree itself looked as if it had once been struck by lightning. At the base the brush was flattened as if someone had sat or knelt there.

He sank to the ground in the same spot where Lydia had been, his thoughts a jumbled mass of confusion. Visions of Travis spun around in his head...memories of a little boy who was Trent's mirror image, a troubled little boy who had grown into a troubled man.

Was there something Trent might have done to circumvent the paths Travis had chosen to travel? Could Trent have been a better brother? These questions had haunted Trent for years and the peace and solitude of his surroundings brought no answers.

The pictures of Travis disappeared as a vision of Elena danced in his mind. Elena, with her lovely eyes and bewitching smile. She was beautiful, but his attraction to her wasn't just a response to her physical appearance. He liked her wry humor, admired the strength he sensed she possessed.

Never had a woman affected him on such a visceral level. Even Joyce, whom he'd thought he loved with every fiber of his being, the woman who he had asked to be his wife, hadn't touched him in the heart places that Elena did.

But were his feelings for Elena honest and good? It was difficult to separate his feelings for her as a woman, and the fact that she was Travis's wife. And this fact alone made Trent's emotions and his desire for her suspect.

At least now that Elena knew of his real identity, she wouldn't come sneaking into his bedroom for a seduction scene. An unexpected wave of disappointment shot through him, followed quickly by a stab of guilt. There was no getting around it…he desired his brother's wife.

But of course it didn't matter that he desired her. Now that she knew the truth, she felt nothing but scorn for him, wanted nothing more than to get him out of her life. For the rest of her life, she would look at him and see the face of the man who had betrayed her.

With a grunt of irritation, he stood and immediately spied what appeared to be a piece of paper folded up and tucked into a crevice in the tree trunk. He plucked it out and unfolded it, his heart racing as he instantly recognized the handwriting from the previous note he'd received.

Travis,

I warned you that if you didn't show up here last night, there would be consequences. I could have killed her, but I didn't.

I know you're mad about our fight in Vegas. I admit, I went a little crazy, but we had a deal and you're trying to cut me out. You know I love you, Travis...but you made me so angry. I'm glad you're all right and your head healed.

I'm going to lie low for the next week. Meet me here one week from tonight. Midnight. Be here with my money or Elena will pay the price for your double cross.

Trent read the note twice, then refolded it and tucked it into his pocket. Walking back to the house, he digested the new information he'd gleaned.

So, the gnarled, lightning struck tree had been Lydia and Travis's meeting place. Not the Roundup, but a tree standing almost in the backyard.

While Elena had sat in the house, watching the clock, wondering where her husband had gone, Travis had been in the copse of trees, meeting his lover and plotting to steal Elena's trust fund.

His heart ached for Elena, who'd been a victim of his brother's lies, betrayed by the man who'd promised to love and cherish her. And if that wasn't enough, Trent himself had deceived her. Was it any wonder she didn't want anything more to do with the Richards brothers?

When he stepped through the back door and entered into the kitchen, she was there. All trace of her earlier tears were gone, replaced by what appeared to be a cool determination to see the farce they were playing through to its completion.

"Lunch will be ready in just a few minutes," she said, not looking at him. "I thought we'd have chicken salad sandwiches." She went to the refrigerator and pulled out a bowl of chicken salad she'd apparently prepared earlier.

He felt the coolness radiating from her. He hadn't realized until this moment how much warmth had emanated from her toward him until now…with it gone.

"I think I might know where Travis is."

That got her attention and she looked at him in surprise. "Where?"

He pulled the note from his pocket and handed it to her. He watched her as she read it, saw the play of emotions that crossed her features. Anger, pain…and finally acceptance. She handed him the note back. "You think he's in Las Vegas?"

He threw the note on the table and sat down. "Yeah. I should have thought about it before. Travis loves Vegas. He tried to get out there at least twice or three times a year. He used to send me postcards, telling me about the fortunes he intended to win while there."

Elena sat down across from him. "I guess he decided it was easier to steal my money than play the odds in Vegas."

Trent fought the impulse to reach out, touch her hand, tell him how sorry he was for his brother's sins. He knew without her saying that she would not welcome even the simplest touch from him.

"If I was to make an educated guess, I'd say that after Lydia stole your money, the plan was for her and Travis to meet in Vegas." He frowned thoughtfully. "They met. Somehow Travis got the money and stiffed Lydia."

Elena picked up the note and read it once again. "It sounds like they had a fight. This says something about his head healing." She frowned and looked at Trent. "I wonder what that means?"

"I don't know. Maybe she coldcocked him...who knows. But, I figure if we want to find Travis...if we want to know what happened, I need to go to Vegas."

Again surprise crossed her features. "Las Vegas is a big city. How would we know where to begin to find Travis? Finding one man would be like searching for a needle in a haystack."

"Not if the needle always hides in the same place." Trent leaned back in his chair, remembering the postcards his brother had sent him over the years. The picture on the front had always been of the same hotel, Sandy's On The Strip. "Travis, up to a point, is a creature of habit. If he's in Las Vegas, I think I know where he'll be staying."

She closed her eyes, looking vulnerable and fragile. Again Trent fought the desire to take her in his arms, somehow soothe away the hurt inflicted upon her by his brother and by himself. But when she opened her eyes, steely strength radiated from their green depths. "When do we leave?"

It was his turn to be surprised. "Elena, you don't have to go. It might be nothing more than a wild-goose chase."

Her eyes became turbulent storm clouds, muddy

green with swirling emotion. "You're right. I don't have to go, but I want to. If Travis is there, I deserve the chance to confront him." She raised her chin, her lower lip trembling for a brief moment. "I deserve the chance to tell him all he lost by not loving me and loving my money instead."

She stood, her chair shooting backward with her motion. "I've had quite enough of other people being in control of my life. I knew something was wrong with my marriage in the first month Travis was here...but I sat and did nothing, hoping it would all work itself out. I'm finished with doing nothing. Now, I'll ask you again...when do we leave?"

A flicker of admiration shot through him as he saw her determination, her desire to face the man who had wronged her...a man she had loved and married. "I'll get on the phone right away and see if we can get a flight first thing in the morning."

She nodded, instantly averting her gaze...as if she couldn't stand to look at him. And was it any wonder? After all, he looked exactly like the man who had betrayed her...identical to the man who had broken her heart.

"I think that's everything," Elena said as she set her small suitcase next to Trent's duffel bag near the front door. "I called Cameron and asked him to feed the horses so they will be taken care of while we're gone. He's also looking after Spooky." She frowned, wondering if there was anything she had forgotten, anything left unattended before they took off for the airport in Billings.

"We shouldn't be gone more than a day or two,"

Trent said as if to allay any worries. "If Travis isn't at the hotel where he normally stays, then we'll come back. There will be no point in looking for him. It would be like looking for that proverbial needle."

They both jumped as a knock fell on the door. Elena answered it to see Millie. The woman looked like a demented Carmen Miranda, with plastic fruit threatening to spill over the brim of her oversized straw hat. "Elena...dear. How are you? I just stopped by to see how the two of you were getting along." Her sharp gaze darted past Elena and focused on the two suitcases. "Oh, are you going somewhere?"

Before Elena could think of an answer, Trent placed an arm around her shoulder and smiled at Millie. "As a matter of fact, we're heading to Las Vegas for a second honeymoon."

Millie clapped her hands together. "Isn't that just wonderful," she gushed. "I should have guessed you two would do something like this. It was so obvious the night of the dance that there was something really special between you two."

Elena felt the heat that worked up from her toes, throughout her body and finally warmed her cheeks. That night she, too, had believed there was something special going on. That night she'd believed there was a chance for a future with the man she had married. That had been the night she had fallen in love all over again with Travis, only to discover he wasn't her husband at all, but rather a counterfeit.

"So tell me, are you going to renew your vows in one of those tacky little wedding chapels?" Millie asked.

"We haven't decided yet," Trent replied. "We're going to play it all by ear when we get there."

"Truly, you must do the chapel thing," Millie exclaimed. "And be sure and get pictures so I can run them in my column."

She shook her head, a plastic pear vibrating with the motion. "I so adore Las Vegas."

As Millie droned on about her favorite hotels in Las Vegas, Elena tried to ignore the evocative pleasure of Trent's arm securely around her. She fit perfectly against the shelter of his body and his pleasant scent enveloped her.

She warmed as she remembered the way his lips had played on hers, the feel of his hands roaming over her heated flesh, the way their bodies had fit together, as if made for each other.

"I hate to be rude," Trent said as he dropped his arm from around Elena. "But we really need to be on our way if we're going to catch our flight."

"Of course," Millie replied. "I don't mean to keep you. I hope you both have a wonderful time." She bobbed her head, a plastic banana falling askew over one eye. She knocked it back in place with the back of her hand, gave them a cheerful wave, then left.

"Guess who will be the leading story in her next column," Elena said the moment the older woman got back in her car. "I can see it now…Mustang's Newest Newlyweds Share Intimate Honeymoon After Tragic Disappearance."

Trent shrugged. "Couldn't be helped. I didn't want to tell her we were on our way to Las Vegas to find your missing husband. I'm sure that would have caused far more problems than we need." He picked up the two bags. "Are you ready?"

"Yes." Elena's nerves gave a tiny jump as they walked outside. She was leaving the security of her home to venture to a city to seek the man she'd married.

Minutes later they were in the car, headed for the airport in Billings. Elena had spent a restless night, her mind playing and replaying her brief relationship with Travis, and her equally brief time with his brother.

She had known. Someplace in the deep unconsciousness of her thoughts, she had known that Trent wasn't Travis. There was a wildness to Travis that wasn't apparent in his brother. Millie had noticed it first...the absence of a wicked gleam in Trent's eyes.

She turned and looked at Trent. So like Travis...yet so unlike him. She had loved Travis. Before they married, while he'd been courting her. She'd believed the love that had shone from his eyes, had fallen into the spell of his romantic words, his sensual passion. And it had all been a lie. Nothing but a lie to lull her while his partner in crime absconded with her trust fund.

She shot another surreptitious glance at Trent. Two peas in a pod? Despite the fact that he seemed different than Travis, they shared the same genes, something Elena could never forget. Two peas in a pod? Or diametric twins?

"It must have been fun being twins. Did your mother dress you and Travis alike when you were young?"

He frowned, as if his memories weren't necessarily pleasant ones. "Yeah. We were dressed alike until the sixth grade. But Travis hated it. He always made sure he had something in his book bag to make him different than me…a kerchief, a hat, a different shirt. Travis truly hated being a twin.''

"What about you? Did you hate it?'' she asked.

He shrugged. "No. I liked the idea of it…you know, having somebody who was exactly like me. But I learned fairly early that Travis might look like me, but that's where the similarities ended.''

"So it was a case of good twin, bad twin?''

He shook his head and shot her a quick smile. "It wasn't as black and white as that. Travis was always into trouble, but nothing major. He was adventurous, bold and just crazy enough to try anything once.''

"You sound like you envy him,'' Elena said softly.

He sighed. "Maybe I did just a little when we were growing up. Everyone loves a daredevil. I was always too apprehensive to do the things he did. I was quieter, less outgoing than Travis.''

"Was he as charming when he was little as he was when I met him?''

Trent laughed, a small burst of wry amusement. "Oh, yes. Trent could charm the birds from the trees. That's what kept him from getting in too much trouble. In high school, he never had less than three girlfriends at a time. Even if one found out about the others, he somehow managed to make it so she wasn't angry with him.''

"What about you? Did you have dozens of girlfriends in high school?'' she asked curiously.

"Not really. All the girls were crazy about Travis. He was the school's bad boy. I was always second choice with the girls.'' He paused a moment, then shot her a look of curiosity. "I've never understood why women are drawn to bad boys.''

"I never was before Travis.'' She leaned her head

back against the seat and stared out the side window. She couldn't explain to him the attraction, wasn't sure she understood it herself.

Travis had possessed an intensity that had left her breathless. He'd had a touch of wildness about him, an edge of mystery that had been magnetic. He'd made her forget the pain of her parents' deaths, had filled her days and nights with excitement.

He was like a fire, burning hot and out of control. Exciting, exhilarating, but she'd quickly learned that living every day with a conflagration was exhausting.

She closed her eyes, a wave of anguish sweeping through her. Her marriage was over. She didn't mourn for Travis, but she did grieve for the loss of her dreams. Rubbing a hand over her stomach, sorrow filled her, sorrow for the child she carried who would not have the pleasure of a father's love and support.

Finally she mourned the fact that the man she'd lived with for the past week, the man who had given her back her hopes, renewed her dreams, was not her husband.

"Elena? Are you okay?" Trent's voice cut into her thoughts.

She opened her eyes and looked at him. "Yes, I'm fine. Why?"

"You were rubbing your stomach. I thought maybe you had a pain or something."

"Yes, I have a pain, but it's not in my stomach. It's in my heart." She looked down at her hand, where her wedding band sparkled in the sunlight. She twisted the gold band off her finger and dropped it on the floor. "What your brother did to me was an outrage."

He nodded, his features taut and strained. "I know."

She stared at him for a long moment as a sudden

thought filled her head. He'd asked her not to go to the sheriff, to give him two weeks to sort things out.

Was it possible he was trying to save Travis from a jail sentence? Did Trent think he could charm her into letting his brother go free?

"Trent, you understand what Travis did is a crime. He might be able to charm the birds out of the trees, but he can't charm me into not pressing charges against him. There will be consequences he'll have to face."

"He'll go to prison," Trent replied, his voice as strained as his facial features.

"You realize that in helping me, you're tightening a noose around his neck? Can you live with that?"

He turned and looked at her, his eyes dark and haunted. "I don't know," he softly replied.

Chapter 10

Elena slept for the duration of the plane ride from Billings to Las Vegas. Trent sat next to her, watching her sleep and thinking about the conversation they'd had in the car.

He'd known on some cerebral level that Travis would have to pay for his crime, but it wasn't until Elena had said as much that Trent felt it on an emotional level.

His brother had finally wronged the wrong woman. He'd crossed over the line of bad behavior into criminal conduct. Trent's feelings where his brother was concerned had always been complex. A dichotomy of joy and sorrow, of admiration and scorn, of love and hate.

Trent knew that somehow in the past week with Elena, he'd subconsciously weighed his duty and responsibility to his brother against the innocence of Elena and the baby she carried. Travis had lost. Trent couldn't live with himself if he allowed Travis to just walk away from this particular situation. What scared him was that he wasn't sure he could live with himself if he were the one responsible for putting Travis behind bars.

Trent knew his brother would probably die in prison, that there was no way Travis could survive months or years in the structure and confinement of a penitentiary. He'd either lose his mind...or die.

There would be no winners in this, no matter how it turned out, he thought. Travis had played a game of chance that had backfired and he had only himself to blame for whatever consequences he had to face. And that's what Trent had to keep remembering.

He breathed a deep sigh as the captain came over the intercom system, requesting that all seats be returned to their upright position in preparation of landing.

He turned and gently touched Elena's shoulder. She stirred, her eyes opening as a sleepy smile curved her lips. For just a split second, it was as if she forgot where she was and who he was. Her eyes were dewy green with drowsy pleasure and an electrical pulse of desire shot through Trent.

"We're getting ready to land. You need to put your seat belt on and straighten your seat," he said.

His voice apparently caused the last of her sleep to fall away. The dewy green of her eyes hardened to something cold and distant and the smile faded from her lips. Trent instantly felt bereft, as if a dark gray cloud had suddenly stolen the warmth of the sun.

It took nearly thirty minutes for them to land then claim their luggage and make their way through the maze of the Las Vegas airport. Once outside they hailed a taxi to take them to Sandy's On The Strip.

"I've never been here before," Elena said as she practically hung out the window in an effort to see all the sights. Hot desert air poured into the open window but she didn't seem to mind, so intent was she on gawking. "Have you been here before?"

Trent smiled, grateful that she seemed to have forgotten her pain momentarily. "Yeah, several times." His honeymoon was to have taken place in Vegas. He had booked the honeymoon suite at the Flamingo for him and Joyce following their wedding ceremony. But the wedding had never taken place, and he'd canceled the honeymoon suite reservation.

As the taxi started down the strip where nearly all the major casinos were, Elena gasped aloud. "I've never seen so many beautiful buildings!" she exclaimed.

"Wait until you see it at night with everything lit up. It's the tackiest—yet the most exciting—display of electricity you'll ever see."

"Are there always so many people?" she asked as the taxi slowed for pedestrians at a crosswalk.

"We're here in the off-season. If you were to come back in a couple of months, there would be a lot more people."

Trent settled back against the seat, watching her as she looked out the window. The sun played havoc with her hair, transforming the dark locks into strands of shining chestnuts and mahogany.

Clad in a pink sundress that bared her shoulders, she looked cool and comfortable and beautiful. Again Trent found himself wondering how his brother had managed so easily to walk away from her.

Sandy's On The Strip was a tiny hotel shoved between two giants. The marquee lacked the flash and glitter of the other hotels, but the lobby looked neat and clean and the desk clerk who greeted them smiled in easy friendliness. "Welcome to Sandy's. Do you have reservations?" he asked.

"No. No reservations," Trent replied. He frowned. Somehow he'd hoped he'd walk in here and the desk clerk and maids would instantly recognize him as Travis.

"How long will you be staying?"

"One night, maybe two." Trent looked at Elena. They hadn't discussed room arrangements.

"The only thing we have available is a double," the clerk said as he punched buttons on a computer keyboard. "In fact it's the last room left. We have several conventions in town and lucky for you somebody canceled about an hour ago."

"That's fine," Elena answered without looking at Trent.

Within minutes they were registered and handed the key to room three-fifteen. The room was small, decorated in gold and brown with two double beds. Elena set her suitcase on the bed closest to the window and Trent placed his bag on the one nearest the door.

"Okay. We're here. Now what do we do?"

"We start asking people if they have seen Travis," Trent replied. "I was hoping the desk clerk would recognize me as him. But it didn't appear he'd seen me before."

"Maybe somebody else who works here will recognize you."

"Maybe." Trent looked at his wristwatch. "Why

don't we go get a late lunch, then we can come back here and start asking questions?''

"Sounds good. I'm famished.''

They ate at a buffet and lingered over coffee, as if reluctant to begin what they'd come for. "Travis told me he was raised on a ranch,'' Elena said as she stirred sugar into her coffee. "Was that just another one of his lies?''

"No. That was the truth. My parents owned a ranch in southern California until we were about fifteen, then they sold it and moved to the city.'' Trent remembered those days on the ranch fondly. He'd loved ranch life, working with the livestock and spending time outdoors.

"How did you become a private investigator?'' she asked.

"I kind of fell into it by accident. I had decided to become a cop and went through the police academy. When I finished that, a friend of my mother's offered me a position with his private investigation firm. I decided to give it a try. Last year I bought him out and he retired.''

"Do you like doing it?''

"Sometimes I love it and sometimes I hate it.''

"That's what Cameron says about bounty hunting. He says you see the best and the worst of people. Only in his case, I think he's seen too much of the worst.''

Trent nodded. "I can relate to that. I've been on the verge of burnout for months. The time at your ranch has felt good. Three years ago I had plans to buy a ranch of my own.''

"What happened?'' She nodded at the waiter who appeared at their table with a coffee pot.

Trent waited until he'd refilled their cups and left

before he spoke again. "Travis happened." He took a sip of his coffee to wash away the unexpected bitterness his memories evoked. "I was engaged to a woman named Joyce. Our plans were to get married and buy a ranch where we could begin our life together. Three days before the wedding Travis seduced Joyce. He bragged to me about it, said as usual I was getting his leftovers. I confronted Joyce and she admitted she'd slept with him. The idea of marriage and a ranch suddenly lost its appeal."

Trent was surprised to discover that the hurt Joyce had inflicted was gone, but the sense of betrayal where Travis was concerned remained.

He was even more surprised when Elena reached her hand out and covered his. "I'm sorry, Trent. That must have hurt dreadfully."

"Yeah, it did. But no more than the pain he has inflicted on you."

She released her hold on his hand and shrugged. "I think betrayal by somebody you love is the worse kind of hurt there is."

"The betrayal is all mixed up with contradictory emotions," he agreed. "Like responsibility and duty…"

"And love," she added.

"Yes. And love." He wondered how long her love for his brother would haunt her. Trent knew as well as anyone that betrayal didn't automatically smother love. Love could flourish in spite of betrayal. "Shall we get back to the hotel?"

"Yes. I'm more than ready for some answers," she agreed.

It was nearly four o'clock when they returned to the

hotel. The same clerk who had checked them in was still behind the front desk. "Excuse me," Trent said. "This is going to sound really crazy, but we're looking for my twin brother. We believe he's either staying here now or has been here in the last several months. Is it possible you might have seen him?"

The clerk shook his head. "I haven't seen anyone who looks like you, but I just started working here a week ago."

"Is there somebody we could talk to who might know if a man looking like me has stayed here?"

The clerk frowned thoughtfully. "We've had a lot of turnover in personnel lately. The hotel was sold a month ago and the new owners pretty well cleaned out the old personnel."

"Surely there's somebody who has worked here for a few months," Elena protested.

The clerk shrugged. "Some of the kitchen help, and a few of the maids, but they don't have much to do with the guests."

Elena looked at Trent. "Maybe one of the maids noticed him." She turned to the clerk. "Would you just check your reservation book and see if he's been here in the last month or so?"

"Ma'am, I can't do that. It's management policy to keep that information confidential." The clerk shrugged. "I don't think I can help you."

"Is it all right if we speak to the maids? See if any of them know of him?"

"Fine with me as long as you don't interfere with their work schedules. The break room is down in the basement. That would probably be the best place to speak with any of the personnel."

"Thank you," Trent replied, then he and Elena headed for the elevators.

"I don't know why he couldn't just look in the register and let us know if Travis had been here," Elena exclaimed as they got into the elevator and Trent punched the button for the basement.

"Most of the hotels and casinos have the same sort of policy of protection for their guests. I would have been surprised if the clerk had looked in his book and given us any information."

"If anyone would have noticed a man who looked like you, it would be a maid," Elena observed. "A woman notices a good-looking man and you and Travis are what most women would consider hunks."

"And if I know Travis, he couldn't help but flirt with the maids," Trent observed, knowing his brother's weaknesses as if they were his own.

The elevator doors whooshed open and they stepped out. Just ahead of them was an arrow pointing to a door that led to the parking garage. To the right was another door that was marked Employees Only.

Trent pushed through that door, holding it open for Elena. They entered a long hallway. The first door off the hallway led to a storage room. The second led to the laundry area, where washers and dryers hummed and thumped with sheets and towels for the hotel guests. The third doorway was the one they sought.

Before they even reached it, they heard the chatter of people, the tinny sounds of a small radio playing, and the clank of a can of soda descending from a vending machine.

Four men and six women gazed at them as they entered. "You must have taken a wrong turn," one of the men said. He was clad in white pants, white shirt and white apron…apparently kitchen help. "The parking garage is out the other door."

"No mistake," Trent replied. "The clerk at the front desk said we could come down here and ask you all a couple of questions."

"What kind of questions?" A security guard eyed them suspiciously as he poured himself a cup of coffee.

"I'm looking for my twin brother. We think he might be staying here or has stayed here in the past month or so. We need to find him," Trent explained.

"It's very important…a family emergency," Elena added.

"Have any of you seen a man who looks just like me?" Trent asked.

He felt ten pairs of eyes studying him. Slowly, each person shook their head negatively. "Are you sure?" he asked, despair sweeping over him. If Travis wasn't here, there was no telling where he might be. "He might have different color hair, or a mustache…" Trent added.

"Honey, I'd remember somebody who looked like you," one of the maids said with a saucy grin. "Ain't nobody like that been on my floor."

"Mine either," an older woman replied. "But you might check back here tomorrow. A new shift comes on at midnight and maybe one of them will know something."

"Thanks," Trent replied.

He and Elena were silent as they rode the elevator back to the third floor. "Elena, I told you this trip might be a wild-goose chase," he said as they entered their room. "We'll check the break room again tomorrow morning, but if nobody has seen Travis, there's nothing more we can do.''

"I know." She sank down on her bed, shoulders slumped in defeat. "He's probably long gone…out of the country."

Trent sat on the edge of his bed, facing her. "I don't know, but somehow I don't think he's out of the country yet." He raked a hand through his hair in distraction. "I just can't believe Travis would fly out of the States, set up a life in a foreign land, and not contact me in some way before he left. It's just out of his character."

"But Trent, it's been over six months since my trust fund was stolen, over five months since Travis disappeared. Why would he remain here, where there is a possibility he could get caught?"

Trent smiled ruefully. "But that is exactly in his character." Again his hand raced through his hair as he thought of his brother. "Travis is arrogant and it's that arrogance that would keep him near. He'd like the risk of remaining here in the States, of feeling as if he was pulling the wool over everyone's eyes. He'd want to believe he was smarter than the cops, smarter than you and me."

Elena frowned, her lips twisting into a bitter smile. "I can't believe how easily he fooled me. Every night he made love to me, he must have been secretly laughing at my stupidity."

"Not stupidity," Trent protested, his heart aching with the pain that darkened her eyes. He leaned forward, his knees nearly touching hers. His arms reached out with the need to hold her, soothe her. But she leaned backward and he dropped his arms to his sides. "Not stupidity," he repeated, knowing he was foolish to think that his arms could offer her comfort. "You fell in love with him, and you trusted him. That's what people in love do."

"Never again," she said fervently. She stood and grabbed her suitcase. "I think I'll take a quick shower and rest for a little while."

Trent stood as well. "And I think I'll take a little walk, maybe hang out in the lobby and see if Travis just happens to walk by." He knew the odds of that happening were minimal, but he didn't want to sit around in the room while she showered. It was too intimate, too disturbing. "Why don't I come back here about seven and we'll go out and get some dinner?"

"That sounds fine," she agreed, then disappeared into the bathroom.

For a long moment he stood with his hand on the doorknob to leave. Never again, she'd vowed. Never again would she enter into a relationship with trust.

She would never be the same again. Travis had left an indelible scar on her soul. And Trent had deepened that scar with his own game of pretense. Something had been broken inside her. If she were lucky, time might provide the glue to paste it back together again. Time...and distance from the Richards brothers, who had brought the pain to her doorstep.

The sound of water running in the shower filled the air. Before Trent's mind could conjure up a vision of her standing naked beneath a warm spray of water, he left the room.

Elena stood at the window, staring out onto the streets that were lit like daylight despite the fact it was almost eleven p.m.

She and Trent had eaten dinner earlier in the hotel coffee shop. Afterward they had walked through the casino area. Although they both pretended to be watching the gamblers, Elena knew Trent was looking for Travis just as she was.

By ten-thirty Elena had decided to call it a day. They were both dispirited, and she was tired, both physically and mentally. Trent saw her to the door of their room, then told her he would be back in an hour or so.

She knew he'd left to give her time and the privacy to change and get into bed before he came back to the room. Where before his thoughtfulness had touched her, now it irritated her. Before, that consideration and thoughtfulness had been the basis of her hope. The hope that she and Travis would be able to mend the fabric of their marriage, fabric that had been rent apart by lies and neglect.

She wanted to hate Trent, for fooling her, for looking like Travis...for being so damned kind that he made her heart warm despite the ache inside her.

With a sigh of irritation, she drew the curtains tightly closed, shutting out the glitter and shine of Las Vegas at night. The light from the bathroom provided the only illumination as she walked across the room and got into the unfamiliar bed.

She sighed, shifting her body to find a comfortable position on the lumpy mattress, although she knew it wasn't the discomfort of the mattress that would keep sleep at bay. Thoughts of Travis—and of Trent—kept the sweet oblivion of sleep elusive.

She had come dangerously close to falling in love with Trent. She'd already made the mistake of loving the wrong man once. Falling in love with his brother would be like the echo of that initial mistake.

Besides, she was afraid that in her heart the two brothers were forever intertwined—the end result a deep heartache she feared might never cease.

Still, even though she didn't want to love Trent, her feelings toward him were confusingly paradoxical. She wanted to hate him, but couldn't forget how it felt to be in his arms. Despite the fact that she didn't want him to be a part of her life, she couldn't stop thinking about the sweet heat of his kisses, the blazing flame of his hands stroking down the length of her body.

She wanted to hate him...and she hated wanting him.

It was close to midnight when she heard the key card slide through the lock and the door creaked open. She closed her eyes, pretending sleep.

She heard the sound of his cowboy boots brushing against the thin carpeting as he made his way across the room. The boots tapped noisily on the bathroom floor, then the bathroom door closed. A moment later she heard the sound of the shower starting.

Releasing a deep sigh, Elena turned over onto her back. She felt as if she'd lost her entire world in the last two days. She'd kept strong in the months when she hadn't known what had happened to Travis, needing to be strong for the baby she carried.

She didn't feel strong at the moment. She felt achingly alone. Travis had taken from her so much more than her money. He'd taken pieces of her she feared she might never get back.

Trent came out of the bathroom, bringing with him the pleasant scents of soap and shampoo. He turned out the light, plunging the room into complete darkness.

Elena heard the groan of his bed beneath his weight, the rustle of blankets as he moved to get comfortable. Again she thought of the night of the dance, when she'd come to his room and fallen into his arms.

She wanted to be angry with him, for allowing their kisses, for encouraging her caresses when she thought he was Travis. She'd wanted to kiss him, she'd wanted him to make love to her and it hadn't mattered what his name was. She'd wanted to make love to the man who had danced with her, the man who had helped her with the dishes all week and had mended fencing and painted the barn.

Even now, as she listened to the sound of his breathing, smelled the scent that belonged to him, she wanted him. She wished she could crawl into his bed and share sweet, tender lovemaking. For she knew, without a doubt, that Trent would make love the way she wanted…slow and gentle, allowing time for hearts to meld, for souls to entwine.

Horror swept over her as realization struck hard. She had fallen in love with her husband's brother. God help her, she had married the wrong man.

Chapter 11

"**I**'m two minutes older than you and years better than you." Travis laughed, his blue gray eyes gleaming. "Mom and Dad loved me best and the women always chose me first. You're nothing but a shadow of me."

Travis laughed again, the sound taunting as his face melted and transformed into the visage of their mother. "Make peace with your brother, Trent." She laid a hand on Trent's face, her bright blue eyes filled with sadness. "He's a good boy, just a little lost. He's not strong like you. Help him find the way, Trent. He's the son of my heart."

Trent sat straight up, for a moment disoriented as he stared around him. Dawn light seeped around the edges of the curtains, scattering pale strands of illumination into the room. Las Vegas. Now he remembered.

He rubbed a hand down his face and across his jaw, where whisker stubble from the night prickled his skin.

He drew a deep breath as the nightmares replayed in his mind. He remembered only the one he'd had just before awakening, but he knew his sleep throughout the night had been haunted by visions of Travis.

He looked at his wristwatch, noting it was just after six. Easing back down in the bed, he looked over at the double bed next to his.

Elena slept on her back, her hair splayed around her head like a starburst of dark silk. Her mouth was slightly parted and her breathing was deep and rhythmic in slumber. Her long lashes cast shadows beneath her eyes, making her hauntingly vulnerable.

The sheet covered her except for one shoulder, where tanned skin peeked out from around the spaghetti strap of her nightgown. She looked as lovely as he'd ever seen her and he felt the stirring of desire deep in his gut.

It had taken him forever to fall asleep the night before, the torture of her nearness driving him half crazy. He'd been able to smell her sweet scent, hear the whisper of her skin against the sheets each time she'd moved.

He wanted nothing more than to crawl into bed with her. He knew the sheets would be warm with her body heat, her scent would surround him as he awakened her with his lips against hers.

She would be startled at first, but as sleep fell away she would respond to him with the same heat, the same passion she had on that night after the dance. Her hands would trail fire as they caressed across his shoulders, down his back. Her breathing would quicken, hot little gasps of delight against the hollow of his throat.

Heat rushed through him as the fantasy continued,

unfolding unbidden in his mind. He could taste her lips, their honeyed heat, feel the silkiness of her skin as his palms and fingers moved over her. Her eyes would darken to the color of mysterious forests, deep green with desire. And she would moan and urge him closer. "Make love to me," she'd whisper. "Make love to me, Travis."

The fantasy crumbled, torn asunder by a stabbing dose of reality. She was his brother's wife. She'd chosen to love and honor Travis until death. Even though Travis had abused her trust, destroyed their marriage, it didn't mean that Elena would want Travis's shadow.

He got out of bed and padded to the bathroom. A cold shower washed away the last remnants of any lingering desire. By the time he got out of the shower, shaved, dressed and left the bathroom, Elena was awake.

She had pulled the curtains open to allow in the light of day and she stood at the window, clad in a thin robe. She turned as he reentered the room. "I ordered a continental breakfast from room service. I hope that's okay." She moved away from the window and sat at the small table in the corner of the room.

"Sounds good. I could definitely use some caffeine."

She gazed at him. "You look tired. Didn't you sleep well?"

He shook his head and sat down across from her. "Actually, I slept like hell. Nightmares."

She smiled sympathetically. "I never had a nightmare in my life until the weeks after Travis disappeared. In the first few days of him being gone, I had the same nightmare every night."

She laced her fingers together on the top of the table

and stared down at them. "I dreamed that Travis and I...we were... making love up on the ridge, and suddenly he slips over the edge and he's hanging on to me and just as I'm about to go over with him, he lets go and falls."

She shivered, as if the memory of the dream had chilled her to the bone. Forcing a smile, she shrugged her shoulders. "Thankfully I haven't had that particular dream in months." She tilted her head, looking bewitchingly lovely. "Want to share your nightmares with me?"

He shook his head. "Nah. They aren't worth repeating." He fell silent for a moment. "Elena, I want you to know that I'll do what I can financially for you and the baby. I've got a healthy bank account of my own and I'll see to it that you don't want for anything."

"I don't want your money, Trent." Her smile fell away.

"But I want to help," he protested. "I feel like I owe it to—"

"You owe me nothing," she interrupted curtly. She stood and picked up her suitcase from the floor. "I can manage quite well on my own. I don't want anything from you or your brother. I'm going to shower and get dressed." She went into the bathroom.

He heard the click of the lock on the door, the sound reverberating in his head. She wanted nothing from him and it was obvious she didn't fully trust him. Otherwise she wouldn't feel the need to lock the bathroom door.

He got up and prowled the room, irritation a heavy weight in his chest. What did she think? That he'd burst into the bathroom and take her against her will? Did she believe him to be a man without honor?

Why not? Why shouldn't she believe that? Travis had been a man without honor...why should she believe Trent to be any different?

His thoughts were interrupted by a knock on the door. It was the breakfast Elena had ordered. He took the tray and set it on the table, then tipped the young man who had brought it. He closed the door then poured himself a cup of the steaming hot coffee.

He was on his second cup when Elena emerged from the bathroom. She was clad in another sundress, this one a bright coral color that skimmed her body from the shoulders to just below her knees. White sandals adorned her feet and he was surprised to see pearly pink nail polish on her toenails.

For some reason the sight of her painted toenails touched him. She had been so strong, so capable throughout the months of Travis's disappearance. She was determined to build a ranch, raise a child alone and refused any help from him. But the sight of those dainty nails reminded him she was a vulnerable woman, with a woman's vanity and pride.

"Oh good, breakfast. I'm famished." She sat down at the table and reached for a thickly iced raisin Danish. Trent poured her a cup of coffee and placed several packets of sugar in front of her.

"Thanks," she said, as if surprised he remembered she took sugar in her coffee. Through the last two weeks of living with her, he'd learned lots of her little quirks. She always ate her vegetables before she touched her meat. She liked her toast unbuttered but slathered with grape jelly. Yes, he knew a lot of her little quirks, and it bothered him that he wanted to know more.

For a few minutes they ate in silence, the only sounds

the noise outside their room of the hotel coming to life for the day.

"I figure if we check the break room this morning and nobody knows anything about Travis, we might as well catch an early afternoon flight back home," he said when they'd polished off the last of the Danishes and coffee. "There's no point in hanging around here indefinitely."

She nodded. "Okay. Should we go ahead and check out of the room now?"

Trent thought a moment. "Nah, let's wait. We have until noon and that way we don't have to drag our bags around with us or check them with the desk."

"You aren't feeling very positive about this, are you?" she asked, her voice subdued.

He hesitated, then shook his head. "No, I'm not. I walked around the casino floor last night for a couple of hours and nobody seemed to recognize me at all. I can't believe if Travis was here he'd keep such a low profile." He cast her a rueful smile. "I warned you this was probably a wild-goose chase."

"But if we hadn't come, we wouldn't know for sure," she protested. "We had to come, Trent. If nothing else for our own peace of mind."

He knew she was right, but peace of mind was the last thing the trip had accomplished for him. He hadn't known peace of mind from the moment he'd walked to her garden gate and seen her for the first time. He stood abruptly, suddenly eager to be out of the small confines of the hotel room. "Shall we head on down to the break room and see what we can find out?"

She nodded and together they left the room and headed for the elevators. Trent felt weighed down by his hopelessness. What if they never found out what had happened to Travis?

He thought of the life insurance policy Travis had sent to him. Elena was the beneficiary, but the insurance company wouldn't pay out any money unless there was a body. And Trent just couldn't believe Travis was dead. Dammit, he would know if his twin brother had drawn his last breath.

The break room was crowded when they walked in. Different faces from the ones they had spoken with the night before. "Excuse me," Trent said loudly in an effort to get everyone's attention.

A plump white-haired lady at the coffee machine turned around. The moment she saw Trent, her mouth fell open and the cup she held dropped to the floor.

Elena grabbed Trent's arm, her fingernails biting into his skin as the older woman staggered back against the wall, her hand clutched at her heart as her eyes widened in shock.

"Wanda!" A dark-haired young women grabbed her arm and led her to a chair. "Are you all right? Get back. Give her some air!" she demanded as the others pressed closer.

Elena released her hold on Trent's arm and crossed the room. "Ma'am, are you all right?" She crouched down next to the older woman. "Wanda? Is that your name?"

She nodded, blue eyes still widened. "Oh my, what a start he gave me." She drew in a deep breath and looked at Trent. "He looks so much like the man I found in room five-twenty-five," she said to her co-workers.

"The man you found?" Trent moved closer, his pulse quickened in excitement. "What man?"

Wanda shrugged. "I don't know his name or anything. I thought he was dead." She shivered. "I went in to clean the room and I found him. The back of his head was all bloody. I figured maybe he tripped and fell and hit it on something."

"You know what his name was?" Elena asked.

She shook her head. "I called the front desk, and they called the police. They took him away in an ambulance."

"Was he alive?"

"I'm not sure," Wanda replied. "I was so upset about the whole thing I started my vacation that very day. When I got back I didn't ask questions. I just wanted to forget the whole thing."

"Anyone else know what happened?" Trent asked. There was no reply from anyone else in the room. Finally, an older man cleared his throat. Trent looked at him expectantly.

"I can't tell you much more," the man said. "I saw them load the man in the ambulance, but management hushed the whole thing up and wouldn't tell anybody anything. The hotel was getting ready to be sold and they didn't want any publicity."

"When did this all occur?" Elena asked.

Wanda frowned. "Three or four weeks ago, maybe a little longer. I don't know. I've tried to put it all out of my head." She stared at Trent. "Maybe you don't look like him...I can't remember. I don't want to remember."

Trent stepped backward. "Sorry to bother you," he said, motioning Elena to his side. "We were looking for the parking garage but we obviously took a wrong turn."

"Where are we going?" Elena asked as they rode the elevator back to the lobby level.

"To the police station," Trent replied. "Wouldn't it be ironic, if all this time we've been trying to find Travis and the whole time he's been in a Las Vegas jail?"

Elena's forehead puckered with worry. "Trent, that woman said nothing about the police arresting the man. She said it was possible the man was dead."

"I'm telling you Travis isn't dead. I know he's not." He heard the conviction in his own voice, strong and resolute. She didn't understand the twin connection. Despite their differences, in spite of the turmoil in their relationship, there was a core connection between the two.

"I don't know what's going on, but this is the first real break we've had," he said to Elena as they stepped out of the hotel and he flagged down a cab. "If the police don't have him in custody, then maybe they'll know what name he was using and where he went."

"Or perhaps Wanda was mistaken and the man she saw wasn't Travis at all," Elena reminded him. "Wanda said she wasn't sure."

"It was Travis," he replied. "I know it was. I feel it. If they can tell me what name he's using, I'll find him." Adrenaline surged inside him. The scent of his quarry was near. Travis thought he was too good to get caught, but Trent would beat him at his own game.

As a taxi pulled up before them, sickness roiled around in Trent's stomach. Was that what all this was about? Besting Travis? He preferred to think he was chasing Travis because it was the right thing to do…the just thing to do.

He helped Elena into the cab, then got in after her, refusing to dwell on the fact that his motivation for finding his brother might be less than honorable.

Trying to get answers from the police station was a study in futility. Elena could feel Trent's frustration flowing from him as they were directed to talk to first one officer, then another, and another…and still had no answers to the questions they'd asked.

It wasn't until just after noon when the detective who had handled the hotel incident came on duty and Trent and Elena were led into his office.

"What can I do for you?" he asked as he motioned them into two straight-back wooden chairs that faced his untidy desk. "Have we met?" he asked Trent. "You look familiar."

"No. We haven't met. I understand about a month ago you were called to Sandy's On The Strip to investigate a man who'd been hurt," Trent explained.

"He wasn't hurt. He was dead," Detective Flarity said succinctly. "The back of his head had been bashed in and the case is still under investigation." He snapped his fingers. "You know, you kind of look like him." His eyes narrowed. "May I ask what your interest is in that particular case?"

Elena looked at Trent, who seemed undisturbed by the detective's words. She looked back at the detective. "I think it might be my husband. He disappeared over five months ago from our home in Mustang, Montana, and we got a tip he might be here in Las Vegas."

"And what's your name?" Detective Flarity pulled

a sheet of paper in front of him and grabbed a pen from his breast pocket.

"Elena. Elena Richards. And this is Trent Richards, my brother-in-law."

Detective Flarity stood and went to a file cabinet in the corner of his office. He pulled a file, then sat back down at his desk with it opened before him. "The body is listed as a John Doe. The morgue has him on ice pending a confirmation of identity. He was found with five different sets of identification. We checked out each of them and they all appear to be aliases."

He tossed a photo across the desk. It flipped in the air and landed face down in front of Elena. Her breath caught in her chest. Tension soared through her as her hand moved toward the picture.

Until this moment, she hadn't faced the possibility that Travis might really be dead. The last time she'd seen him, he'd been too full of life, too vital to imagine his very existence being no more.

She picked up the photo, her gaze connecting with Trent's. In his gaze she saw hope...utter faith that the picture would not be of his brother.

She looked at the photo and pain stabbed through her. Travis's face, looking waxy and pale, stared back at her. His hair was longer than she'd ever seen it and a mustache rode his upper lip, but there was no mistake. Tears burned as she once again looked at Trent.

He must have seen the truth in her eyes. He reached out a hand that trembled slightly. Reluctantly she gave him the picture at the same time an unexpected sob released itself from her.

He stared at the photo for a long minute, his face completely devoid of expression. The only evidence of his turmoil was a muscle tick near the corner of his left eye. He handed the picture back to Detective Flarity. "That's Travis Richards. That's my brother." He stood and without saying another word, left the office.

Elena jumped up to follow him, tears streaming down her cheeks. She'd been angry with Travis, but she'd never wished him dead. He had been her husband...was the father of her child and despite his betrayal of her, the permanent loss of him ached inside her.

She found Trent outside the police station. He leaned against the adobe building, eyes closed as if in prayer. She touched his arm, startling him.

For a long moment they gazed into each other's eyes, then he grabbed her to him and held her tight. She felt body tremors, but didn't know if they raced through him, or through herself.

Grief rained from her, grief that had built up inside her for almost six months. It didn't matter that she had intended to divorce Travis, his death ached inside her as the baby they had made together kicked and turned as if to protest the loss.

Trent didn't cry. He remained stoic, rubbing her back and holding her tight as she wept. The desert sun bore down on them and passerbys gazed at them curiously. Elena wondered vaguely if they thought she was crying because she'd lost all her money at the gaming tables.

Detective Flarity appeared next to them, his face lined with sympathy. He handed Trent a piece of paper. "If you take that down to the basement, they'll release your brother's property to you."

"I know who killed him," Trent said, his arms still wrapped around Elena. "Her name is Lydia Walsh. She's wanted in Montana. She wrote me a note that refers to Travis's head injury and a fight she had with him in Vegas. She doesn't realize he's dead.''

''You got a phone number and address where you can be reached?'' Detective Flarity asked.

Elena heard Trent give the officer her address and phone number, then Detective Flarity left them alone once again. She pulled away from Trent, her grief momentarily spent.

''I want to get Travis's personal effects,'' he said as he raked a hand through his hair. ''And then I need to go to the morgue and see about having his body brought home. If you don't mind, I'd like to bury him next to my mother in California.''

''That's okay with me,'' she said softly, searching his face intently. He seemed far too controlled and in command considering the circumstances. She sensed a grief too deep for tears within him.

''If you want, you can go on back to the hotel room. I can take care of the rest of it.''

She shook her head. ''No, I'll come with you.'' She couldn't explain it to him, but she was afraid for him. She feared the moment when he allowed his emotions to finally be released.

It took only a few minutes to get Travis's personal effects. There were three wallets, each with a full set of false identification. Credit cards, passports, driver's licenses...Travis could have traveled anywhere under any of the five names they found on the paperwork.

They also were handed a bank book from a Swiss bank account. Elena suspected the account would have both her money and Cam's in it. Although the officer explained to her that the police had frozen the account until Travis's murder was solved and the case was closed.

From there, they went to the city morgue where Trent made the arrangements for the transportation of the body to the funeral home that would take care of placing Travis in a final place of rest.

They were quiet on the way back to the hotel. It was after five and they decided to catch an early morning flight home the next day. They ate dinner in the hotel coffee shop, Trent picking at a hamburger and Elena nibbling on a salad.

"I'm going to take a walk," Trent said after they'd finished eating. "You go ahead to the room." He touched her cheek lightly. "You look exhausted. I'll be up to the room later."

An hour later Elena stepped out of the shower and changed into her nightgown. As she had showered, she'd tried to imagine how she'd have felt had it been Cameron's picture, Cameron's body waiting to be identified. The horror had been unimaginable and had started tears flowing once again.

It wasn't until she was in bed that she realized she had taken on Trent's grief as her own. The tears he'd been unable to shed, she'd shed for him. Her heart ached not only with her own pain, but with his as well.

Tomorrow she would be back home...home on the ranch where she belonged. She'd raise her child alone and when he or she got old enough to ask questions about their father she would lie. She would say that he had been a man who loved life. She wouldn't say he'd stolen her money and left her and had died in a gaudy Las Vegas hotel, killed by his accomplice in crime.

By this time next week Trent will have met Lydia

and hopefully she would be behind bars. This particular painful chapter of Elena's life would be over...only scars left to tell the tale.

She fell asleep almost immediately, exhausted by the turmoil and anguish the day had brought. She awakened suddenly, unsure what had pulled her from her dreamless sleep.

Then she heard it. A choked sob muffled by a pillow. She rolled over on her side, barely able to see in the faint illumination that Trent was in his bed. Finally his grief had struck.

She remained still, knowing he thought she was asleep and his mourning was occurring privately. Another deep sob tore from him, a sound so profoundly anguished that Elena felt its echo in every chamber of her heart.

She remained still, unsure what to do. She didn't want to intrude on his anguish, but she had too much compassion to lie here and listen to him grieving alone.

"Trent?" She sat up.

"It's okay, Elena. Go back to sleep," he said, his voice raspy with thick emotion.

But she couldn't go back to sleep, couldn't ignore the fact that he hurt. He'd held her so tight, soothed her with his touch, when she had hurt.

She got out of her bed and went to his. He tried to turn away from her, as if unable to abide her seeing him. But she wouldn't let him escape her. She wrapped her arms around him, pulling him against her length and cradled his face in her hands.

His bare chest burned as if he were fevered, but she knew it was the fever of anguish that made his skin feel hot.

"I thought I would know," he said with a choked sob. His eyes were gray pools of pain. "I was certain I would know in my heart if he was gone. And he's been gone over a month and I didn't know it. I didn't feel it." He closed his eyes but tears seeped out beneath his lids, trekking down his cheeks in trails of sorrow.

She swept at the tears with her fingers, but said nothing, knowing no words would comfort. She knew from experience that he needed to mourn. Tears were far healthier when they were cried than when they were kept inside.

He opened his eyes and gazed into hers. "I always knew in my heart something like this would happen to him. I think my mother knew it as well. The last thing she said to me before she died was to find Travis and make peace with him. He was my parents' favorite. Did I tell you that before?"

She shook her head, knowing the stream of consciousness coming from him was his way of dealing with his grief. She remained silent and let him continue to talk.

"Travis was everyone's favorite despite his faults. He could make you feel more alive than you ever dreamed possible. But, I guess you know that. You loved him, too."

She knew now wasn't the time to tell him that she'd long ago fallen out of love with Travis. Trent didn't need to hear that now.

He reached up and cradled her face in his palms, much as she did his. He moved his thumbs to play across her lips. "I'd hoped that there would be time for redemption for Travis, hoped that loving you would save him, and if that didn't work then maybe I could finally save him...." His voice cracked and a deep sob wrenched through him. Again he closed his eyes and twisted his head so he could turn away from her.

"Trent..." She took hold of his chin and forced him to turn back to her. "Nobody could save Travis but Travis. He chose his own paths, and you can't be responsible for the choices he made."

He shook his head. "I know, but it doesn't make the hurt any less."

She nodded, her heart breaking for the twin who had died, but more so for the one left behind.

She didn't know if it was right or wrong, didn't care in any case. She only knew her instinct was to kiss him and so that's what she did.

She pressed her lips against his and his response was instantaneous...and much more than she'd anticipated. He responded with a ravenous hunger.

His tongue swirled into her mouth, dancing with her own as his hands moved down the length of her, burning through the thin material of her nightgown.

"Elena...Elena..." he moaned against her lips as the kiss ended. "I want you."

Elena froze, her heart thudding a frantic rhythm. Trent released her immediately, as if afraid he'd stepped over a line. And he had. And she was about to do the same. "I want you, too," she whispered.

Chapter 12

What had begun as an attempt to comfort, quickly blossomed into something far more intense and exquisitely more pleasurable.

With a groan, Trent gathered Elena into his arms, his kiss stealing her breath with the magnitude of his hunger. And she responded with a hunger of her own.

His mouth was hot…needy…and she welcomed the heat, reveled in the need. It had been so long…so achingly long since she'd been held, been kissed.

His lips left hers and instead trailed fire across her cheek. She closed her eyes and moaned softly as he kissed behind her ear, then nipped and licked down the length of her neck.

She tangled her hands in his hair, enjoying the rich softness as it coiled around her fingers. It smelled of shampoo and fresh outdoor air.

She moved her hands from his hair to his broad back.

Where before his skin had felt fevered, it now felt as if an inferno burned deep within him.

She stroked her hands across the width, felt the play of muscles against her fingertips. She traced a small ridge of scarred flesh in the center of his back, wondered vaguely what had happened to cause the scar.

As his mouth moved back up to hers, she lost herself in him, wanting him to kiss her...to love her forever. She ran her hands across the waistband of his boxers, wanting him naked.

He grabbed her hands, brought them up to his lips and kissed them. "Slow, Elena," he whispered. "There's no need to hurry. I want to savor every moment, every touch with you."

There was nothing he could have said or done that would have stoked her desire higher than those particular words. "Yes," she whispered in return. "Yes. Slowly."

He gently maneuvered her onto her back and he lay beside her on his side. He ran a hand lightly over her breasts and across the swell of her stomach. "You are so beautiful," he said, his eyes glowing with a wildness she'd never seen before.

She shivered as his hand cupped one of her breasts. He leaned over and kissed her again, a long, deep kiss that once more threatened to steal all her breath from her. And before she could catch her breath, his fingers began to unfasten the buttons of her nightgown.

He held her gaze as each button came unfastened. When she was unbuttoned to the waist, he pushed aside the fabric, exposing her breasts to his heated gaze. He dipped his head and captured a turgid peak in his mouth, creating a sensory thrill that shot through Elena.

He loved first one breast, then the other, using his mouth and tongue to tease and arouse. He paused only long enough to unfasten the rest of the buttons and pull the nightgown off her shoulders so she was left wearing only a tiny pair of lace panties.

For a moment Elena tensed, wondering if he would find her blossomed belly unattractive. But she needn't have worried. He laid his palms against the swell and pressed his mouth against her stomach as if to kiss the baby within.

He raised his head and gazed at her as his hands gently glided over her swollen stomach. "I've never seen anything so beautiful," he said, his voice filled with awe. "I can feel the life inside you."

Molten heat swirled inside her at his words. Oh, this man was so dangerous to her senses. He seemed to know just what she needed, and gave it easily, willingly. Any fears she'd momentarily entertained faded away beneath the glow of his eyes, the sweetness of his words.

He'd told her she was beautiful, and he made her feel beautiful. She wanted to weep with the glory of it all. It had been so long…so achingly long since she'd been held, been loved. As much as she'd thought she loved Travis, he'd never made her feel so special, so loved.

Once again she plucked at his boxers, wanting to feel his naked flesh next to hers. He accommodated her wish, pulling the shorts down and kicking them off the end of the bed.

She turned over on her side, facing him and reached down to grasp his hot, hard flesh. He gasped at the intimate touch, growing harder…longer in her hand. He pulled away from her with an embarrassed burst of laughter. "I...you'd better not touch me yet...I have little control where you are concerned."

Instead he reached down and stroked her through the thin lace of her panties. She arched upward, a moan escaping her. Just when she thought she could stand it no longer, he swept her panties off and caressed her again, this time taking her to heights of passion she'd never known before.

She hurtled toward the pinnacle of pleasure like a star shooting across the sky. She felt boneless, mindless...nothing more than a mass of sweet sensation. As she reached the top and wave after wave crashed through her, he leaned forward and captured her cries of pleasure with his mouth.

Elena clung to him weakly, tears streaking down her cheeks...tears of joy and pleasure. Within seconds, her hunger was back, more intense than before...the hunger to be possessed, to feel him inside her.

"Trent, make love to me. Please make love to me now," she said.

"I don't want to hurt you, Elena." His voice was thick with emotion as he laid his palm against her stomach.

She smiled. "The only way you'll hurt me is if you don't make love to me."

"Are you sure it's okay?" Still he hesitated.

Once again she reached between them and grasped him in her hand. He groaned, his flesh pulsating with need. He rolled over on top of her, careful to keep the bulk of his weight on his arms.

He entered her slowly, his gaze connected with hers. His eyes reflected the same awe, the same joy that riveted through her as his possession became complete.

As he began to move inside her, she broke the eye contact. She closed her eyes and allowed her thoughts, her sense of self, her very soul to surrender to him.

Afterward, instead of rolling over and going to sleep, he held her in his arms. Although they didn't speak, Elena felt as if their hearts conversed in a language all their own.

He stroked her hair with a languid touch, their bodies remaining close to one another. Never had she been loved so completely and never had she known such sexual contentment.

She wondered if he felt the same. If he'd found her to be a satisfying partner. Travis had always made her feel inadequate, as if she couldn't do enough to please him. Not that it mattered. She knew she and Trent would not make love again.

She knew eventually they would both have to face reality. And reality was that they had been brought together by a man who would always remain between them.

She'd married Travis and carried his baby. And it was possible when the smoke cleared from all this, Trent would always see his brother's death when he looked at her.

Elena also knew that had grief not clouded their judgments, this night would have never happened. She had caught Trent at a vulnerable moment, when he'd needed to be held, to be loved. And she had been in that same place of vulnerability, needing him to chase away her sadness with breathtaking passion.

But she didn't want to think of all that at this moment. For now she was content to lie in Trent's arms, bask in the glow of being sated by a thoughtful, selfless lover. They would face the aftermath of their lovemaking tomorrow when they got back to the ranch.

She closed her eyes, allowing the rhythmic beat of Trent's heart to lull her to sleep.

"Joyce and I had a great time last night." Travis smiled slyly and Trent's heart skipped a beat. "She said you're a good lover, but I'm better." Travis punched him lightly in the shoulder. "Face it, little brother. All the women love me, even your women." He walked away, his laughter filling the air.

Trent gasped and came awake, his heart pounding with anxiety. As the nightmare faded, leaving only a taste of bitterness in his mouth, he became aware of his surroundings.

One of his arms was sound asleep and trapped beneath Elena. Her hair splayed across his face, tickling with each breath he took. Using the hand he had free, he pushed aside her hair, marveling at the silken feel of each strand.

He looked toward the windows and realized it was well after dawn. Bright daylight snuck in around the edges of the curtains. They should get up, check out of the room and get to the airport. It was time to go back to the ranch.

Still, he remained unmoving, reluctant to wake her up, reluctant to leave the warmth of the covers, the warmth of her body against his.

She had been a passionate lover, just as he'd thought she would be. With her deep kisses and sweet caresses, she'd taken his grief and transformed it into desire.

But this morning the taste of grief was once again in his mouth, Travis's death weighed heavy in his heart.

He wished he could make love to Elena again, lose himself once more in the desire she evoked in him. But he knew that would only make things worse. There was a certain shame in the fact that he and Elena had grieved Travis's loss by making love.

Gently he extricated his arm from beneath her, needing to distance himself from the scent of her, the warmth of her. He eased out of the bed and padded into the bathroom.

Staring in the mirror, he saw not his own reflection, but that of his brother's. Identical twins. Two halves of the same fertilized egg.

Had Elena imagined Travis making love to her last night? After all, Travis was the man she'd loved, the man she'd chosen to marry. He'd betrayed her, and he'd died, but that didn't mean Elena's love for him had completely died.

Even if she did no longer love Travis, if his betrayal of her had managed to suffocate any love she had left, it would be impossible for her not to remember that betrayal each time she looked at Trent.

He turned away from the mirror and started the water in the shower. Making love to Elena had been a big mistake. He needed to get her scent off him, forget the sweet taste of her, the feel of her silken skin against his.

As steamy water cascaded down his body, he hoped Elena understood that last night had been an anomaly, a one-time weakness that would not, could not be repeated. There was no sense in fooling himself. Elena now and forever would belong to Travis in Trent's mind. And he would always wonder if that's why he wanted her so badly.

He finished his shower and dressed quickly. Travis's death changed nothing in the plans for the next couple of days. He and Elena would go back to the ranch and pretend to be husband and wife.

They would go to the sheriff and tell him what had happened and hopefully the night that Lydia was to meet him she would instead meet justice. She was not only facing charges of theft, but for murder as well.

Once Lydia was caught and behind bars, Travis's case would be closed, Elena would get most of her trust fund back, the money from the life insurance policy, and Trent would go back to his life in California.

He frowned and ducked his head beneath the spray of water, wondering why the thought of his previous life paled when compared to the life he'd been living for the past two weeks.

Staying at Elena's ranch had reminded him of all the dreams he'd once had. He'd once wanted to live on a ranch, be a modern-day cowboy. He'd had a taste of that at Elena's and now had a feeling he wouldn't be satisfied going back to his former life.

The town of Mustang, with its slow pace and friendly people had captured his fancy, but he wouldn't settle there. There was no way he could live in the same small town as Elena and not want her, despite the fact that wanting her was all wrong.

He stared at his reflection in the mirror one last time, this time seeing only the image of a man who would never be as exciting, as thrilling, as bold and adventurous as his brother. He saw only the shadow of Travis.

With a frown of irritation, he left the bathroom.

"Good morning," Elena said as she sat up and shoved a cloud of hair away from her face.

"Almost afternoon," he replied, wishing she didn't look so damned sexy, with her hair in charming disarray and the sheet slipping down to reveal a tanned shoulder and the curve of one rounded breast. "I hope you can be ready to check out in half an hour, otherwise we get charged for another night in the room."

"Sure…okay," she said, her frown making him realize he'd been more curt than he'd intended. She started to get out of the bed, then paused, pink color rushing to her cheeks.

"Why don't I go on down to the front desk and get us checked out." He realized despite their lovemaking the night before, she was embarrassed to get out of bed naked while he stood and watched.

For some reason, her unexpected burst of modesty touched him. He smiled gently. "Why don't we meet at the front desk and we'll get some breakfast before we head out for the airport."

She returned his smile with a sunshine one of her own. He felt the warmth of it in the pit of his stomach. "I'll see you downstairs," she said.

He stepped out of the room and breathed a deep sigh. The remaining five days with her before his rendezvous with Lydia may be more difficult that he'd initially believed.

Five days of pretend husband-and-wife. Five days that would have been so much easier if he hadn't made love to Elena last night. Five days of remembering her hot kisses, her throaty moans. Five days of concentrating on not making the same mistake twice.

It didn't take him long to check them out of the room. He sat in the lobby to await Elena, trying to keep his thoughts away from Travis. He was grateful his father and mother were gone, that neither of them were alive to bury a son. It wasn't the natural order of things for parents to bury their children.

Nor was it the natural order for a child to be raised without two parents. Now that he knew his brother would have no part of his child's life, Trent was surprised to realize he wanted a part in the child's life.

There would be no other nieces or nephews for him, and he seriously doubted if he would have children of his own. He wanted to share some part, no matter how small, of the life of the child Elena carried. The baby was the last of the Richards line...a legacy for the future.

He broached the subject to Elena as they ate breakfast in the coffee shop. "Elena, you told me the night I confessed my real identity to you that you wanted nothing from me. But I want something from you."

She gazed at him warily. "What do I have that you could possibly want?"

"I want to be an uncle to the child you're carrying. I want to be an active participant in his or her life." He held up a hand as if to still any protest she might make. "Elena, that baby is the last of my family. You told me you'd had enough of the Richards...but that baby is a Richards. Let me be a part of its life, let me tell the baby the things I know about its father."

"What things would you say about Travis?" she asked softly, appearing genuinely curious.

Trent stirred his coffee thoughtfully, surprised by the sudden emotion that welled up inside him. Visions from the distant past rose up, haunting him with what once had been and never would be again. "I'd say that when Travis was ten years old he could throw the best knuckleball in the entire fifth grade. I'd say that Travis could throw a rock across a pond and make it skip at least four times before it sank to the bottom.''

He heard the shaky timbre of his voice and swallowed hard for control. ''I'd tell about the time Travis socked Big Arnie Walton in the nose because Arnie called me stupid and the way Travis could sing 'Silent Night' so sweetly he made angels weep.'' He looked at Elena and saw tears sparkling in her eyes.

''I wish I could have known that Travis,'' she said softly.

He laughed self-consciously and drew in a deep breath. ''I'd nearly forgotten him.'' Once again he looked down at his coffee cup. ''He could have been so much...done so much, if he'd just made different choices in his life.''

Elena reached across and touched his hand gently. ''I'd like it if you are a part of the baby's life.'' She pulled her hand back and placed her napkin beside her plate. ''Shouldn't we be getting to the airport?'' she asked, letting him know she didn't want to talk anymore about Travis.

They didn't talk about the night they had shared until they were in the car driving home from the Billings airport. And then it was Elena who brought it up. ''Trent...about last night,'' she began.

''Elena, things got a little crazy last night. Emotions were running high and we were both vulnerable.'' He tightened his grip on the steering wheel, not looking at her. ''I'll be staying at your place until the meeting with Lydia. It's important that we keep up the appearance of a happily married couple, but I can promise you last night won't happen again.''

"I know," she said, her voice a mere whisper.

He cast her a surreptitious glance. She stared out the window as if lost in thought and he wondered if she was thinking about Travis...missing him and wishing he were here.

He relaxed, grateful that she understood that last night had been a mistake. Beautiful, but a mistake nonetheless. For this last week of them being together, things would be much less complicated if they both understood the rules.

"I'm supposed to meet Lydia next Tuesday night by the old gnarled tree in the timber north of the house. Sometime before then we need to get to the sheriff's department and set up an ambush."

His words seemed to snap Elena from her reverie. She looked at him worriedly. "Maybe you shouldn't meet her. We know now she's capable of violence. She killed Travis."

"I have to meet her," he countered. "She's like a rat hiding in a hole where nobody can find her. Only one thing brings her out of her hole...cheese. In this particular case, I'm the cheese. If we're going to catch her, I have to be the bait."

"She scares me," Elena replied. "She's risked everything for my money and for Travis. She obviously believes Travis betrayed her...you know what they say about a woman scorned."

"I want her caught. I want to see her pay for Travis's death. And when she's caught, don't forget you will see most of your money returned to you."

She waved her hand dismissively. "I told you before, the money never really mattered to me." Her forehead wrinkled with a frown. "The sad part in all of this is that it was all so unnecessary. If all Travis wanted was my money, all he had to do was wait two years. The money would have been released to me and as my husband he would have had access to it all. If he'd just been patient, I would have given him what he wanted anyway.''

Her words reminded Trent that Travis had owned Elena's heart. She would have shared with Travis all she had because she'd loved him.

''It's nice to be home,'' she said a moment later as he turned down the gravel road that led to her place.

Trent felt a sense of homecoming as the ranch came into view. The newly painted barn rose proud and tall. The house looked sturdy and warm despite the need for new paint. ''There's a few more things I'd like to get down around the place before I leave,'' he said.

''You don't have to do anything more, Trent,'' she protested. ''You've already done too much.''

''I don't mind. In fact, I enjoy the work. Besides, I'm not just doing it for you, I'm doing it for my niece or nephew as well.'' He parked out front and they got out of the car.

Elena went to the front door, where she was greeted by Spooky's barks. She unlocked the door and opened it and the little black poodle darted out, dancing and jumping in the air with joy. Spooky ran first to Elena, then to Trent, her little tongue licking as if both were gigantic dog biscuits.

''You know, I should have known you weren't Travis on that first day when you arrived and Spooky loved you.'' Elena sat down on one of the porch chairs, watching as Spooky ran circles around Trent.

Trent laughed at the poodle's antics as he opened the

trunk of the car to remove their bags. He turned at the sound of hooves pounding the dry ground.

"Oh look, it's Cameron," Elena said. "He must have seen our car pull in."

Trent set the bags on the ground and straightened as Cameron reined his horse to a sudden halt before him. In the blink of an eye Cameron flew off his horse and toward Trent.

"You bastard," he exclaimed.

Trent watched in amazed shock as Cam's fist shot out and caught him on the right side of his jaw. His head snapped back and he stumbled to the ground. He was vaguely aware of Elena's surprised scream.

As he saw Cameron approach once more, a blood rage in the man's eyes, Trent shot up and raised his own fists. "You hit me again and I'll tear your head off," he said.

"Cameron, stop it. What are you doing?" Elena cried.

"Elena. This man isn't your husband. He's Travis's brother. He's been playing house with you under false pretenses." As if his own words sparked a renewed burst of rage, Cameron raised his fists again and advanced on Trent.

"She knows that, you crazy cowboy," Trent exclaimed.

"He's right, Cam. I know he's Trent and not Travis. Come inside and we'll explain it all to you," Elena said.

Cameron stared at first one, then the other. Slowly he lowered his fists. "Sorry about that," he said to Trent.

"No problem," Trent replied. At the same time his fist shot out and connected with Cam's jaw.

Chapter 13

"**H**ow did you find out who I was?" Trent asked Cameron when the dust had cleared and Elena had corralled both men inside the house and to the kitchen table.

"The grocery store in town complained to the sheriff about a car that had been parked in their lot for the last two weeks. I happened to be in the sheriff's office when the call came in. He got the license plate number and discovered it was registered to a Trent Richards."

Cameron frowned darkly. "Trent Richards...Travis Richards, it seemed too big of a coincidence so I did a little investigating on my own. Discovered Travis had a twin brother and put two and two together."

"Travis is dead," Elena said, unsurprised when her brother showed little emotion. There had been no friendship between the man she had married and her brother. "Lydia Walsh killed him in Las Vegas."

Cameron's eyes flared wide with this information. As Trent filled him in on everything that had happened in the last two weeks, Elena found herself thinking of the conversation they'd had concerning Trent's desire to be a part of the baby's life.

It would be good for the baby to have somebody from Travis's family to love. And Trent knew things about Travis she didn't know...things that would someday be important to a child seeking information about daddy. She wanted him in the baby's life...she wasn't sure she wanted him in her life.

Her feelings for him scared her. She should have never slept with him, for last night, while lying in his arms, she'd realized the depths of her love for him. She loved him as she'd never loved his brother and that scared the hell out of her.

He'd made it quite clear to her that he didn't feel the same. A man who loves doesn't promise not to make love again. For him, last night had probably been a pleasant interlude, a sharing of sorrow in passion's arms. But it hadn't been a pronouncement of love for her.

She had confused passion for love when she'd married Travis. She would never make the same mistake again. Besides, she wasn't sure if her love for Trent might be a trick of her imagination, that he was merely an imitation of the man she'd once believed she'd loved, then had learned to dislike. It was all jumbled up in her head...Trent...Travis...betrayal...and desire. He had the face of the man who had betrayed her, and the heart of a man she could love.

"Elena?"

She started, assuming by the sharpness in Cameron's

voice that he had called her name several times. She shoved away her confusing thoughts and focused on her brother. "Yes?"

"Are you sure this is all right with you? To continue this pretense for the next week in hopes of catching Lydia?"

She nodded, keeping her gaze averted from Trent. "We can't think of any other way to get her."

Cameron eyed Trent, then looked at Elena once again. "I don't know...I don't like it." He leaned back in his chair and looked back at Trent. "No offense, but how do I know you aren't just like your brother? You're certainly the spittin' image of him physically."

Trent appeared to take no offense at the words. He sat forward and met Cameron's gaze squarely. "I'm not my brother, and you'd do well to remember that." He let his words hang in the air for a moment. "I'm here to right a wrong. Hopefully once Lydia is caught, you and Elena will recover some of your trust fund money. Elena has a large settlement coming from a life insurance policy. Financially she'll be fine." His eyes darkened. "And in time, perhaps the emotional scars Travis left behind will heal."

"But who is going to keep Elena safe between now and the night of your meeting with Lydia?" Cameron asked. "You told me Lydia took a shot at her the other day. That sounds pretty damn serious to me."

Trent nodded. "It is."

"I'll be fine," Elena interjected, irritated that the two men were talking over and around her as if she wasn't present. "I'll stay here in the house."

"Maybe for the next week I should help out with the chores around here," Cameron said thoughtfully. "That way I can help keep an eye on things, make sure Lydia Walsh doesn't do anything to threaten Elena.''

Elena started to protest, then closed her mouth. She'd be foolish to turn away Cameron's offer of protection. They had no idea what Lydia might do next...but it would definitely be difficult for her to do anything to Elena if she had to come through two strong men to accomplish it.

"You're sure neither you nor the sheriff said anything to anyone about my real identity?" Trent asked Cameron.

"Sheriff Wilder promised not to say anything to anyone until I had a chance to talk to you and Elena." Cameron looked at his sister. "You know Jesse is crazy about you and wouldn't do anything to cause you grief."

Elena nodded, her cheeks flaming. When she'd first arrived in Mustang she'd dated the handsome sheriff a few times. Although he was a wonderful man, Elena had felt no magic. They'd agreed to just be friends, although Jesse had made it clear he wouldn't mind more.

"It's important nobody know the truth. If gossip gets around, Lydia might hear it and once she hears I'm not Travis, she'll be gone for good," Trent said.

Cameron frowned. "I'd still like to know where she's staying...how she's managing to come and go without being seen."

Trent shrugged. "Who in town knows what she looks like besides you and Elena?"

"I guess nobody," Cameron conceded. He stood, his muscles taut as if he anticipated a fight. Elena knew the look well. Her brother was ready for a hunt. A bounty hunter who suddenly sensed his quarry. "Knowing she's in the area, I'm going to do a little snooping, see if I can flush her out before your meeting with her."

"You don't want to spook her so bad she runs before we can get her," Trent cautioned.

Cameron smiled at him dryly. "I'm a bounty hunter by trade, and I'm very good at what I do. If I find her...she won't get away."

Trent sent him an equally dry smile. "Nor will she get away from me if I find her."

Elena knew it was not a contest between the two men, but rather an acknowledgment that they each had scores to settle with Lydia Walsh.

"Was he as intense when you were growing up?" Trent asked the moment Cameron left.

Elena smiled. "Yes, he was as intense. But he was the best big brother a girl could ever wish for. All my friends were mad about him and no matter how much I tagged along behind him, he never complained."

Trent propped his chin up on a hand and gazed at her thoughtfully. "So you had a good childhood." It wasn't a question, rather a statement of fact. She nodded. "I'll bet you were a cute little girl."

Her cheeks warmed and she laughed. "Actually, I was quite homely as a child. I was horridly skinny and small for my age. My mouth was too big for my face and my nose was too small."

"I can't imagine you not being as beautiful then as you are now." He sat back, as if his words surprised himself as much as they surprised her. He stood suddenly. "I think I'll go out and take a look around, check on the horses and let Spooky run a little."

She nodded, alternately touched and discomfited by his sweet words.

"Come on Spooky," he said as he walked to the back door. The poodle barked with excitement as Trent opened the door and the two of them went outside.

Elena got up from the table and moved to the back window. She watched as Trent and Spooky walked toward the corral, where the two horses whinnied a greeting.

The next five days were going to be difficult ones. If she were smart, she'd ask him to leave right now and let Jesse handle the problem of Lydia Walsh. But she knew the odds of the sheriff finding Lydia's lair were minimal. It made sense to follow through on the plan and wait for Lydia's meeting with Trent.

Trent and Cameron would keep her safe from Lydia. Now all she had to figure out was how to keep her heart safe from Trent.

Trent climbed on the back of Lady, the bigger of the two palominos and took off riding across the pastures north of the house. He needed to ride hard, release the tension that had been building for the past four days.

He and Elena had gone to the sheriff's office the day after they returned from Las Vegas. There, Trent had told the dark-haired Jesse Wilder about the events that had brought him to Mustang, Travis's death and his planned rendezvous with Lydia.

At that meeting, they had devised an elaborate plan to get some of the sheriff's men to the ranch unseen. On the morning of the meeting, Trent and Elena would go into town and shop. Early evening they would drive back to the ranch, with the sheriff and his team hidden in the back of the pickup. Once at the ranch, the men would wait until nightfall, then take up positions in the woods to await the arrival of Lydia.

It sounded foolproof, but Trent knew there was always room for error. Still, it wasn't thoughts of Lydia or the setup for her arrest that had made him antsy.

He urged Lady faster, glad his skills as a rider had returned so easily. Cameron had done a good job with the horse, who responded to the lightest touch of the reins.

His thoughts turned to Elena. Elena. Her name rode the wind as it whistled in his ears. Faster and faster he pushed the horse, as if he could outrun the desire he'd fought against for the last four days. But she was in his head…in his blood…in his heart.

The last four days had been a study in torture. They had fallen into a pattern of unfailing courtesy with one another, a polite uneasiness that seethed inside him. As she made his breakfast, he found himself wanting to kiss her neck until she forgot about bacon and eggs, or sausages and pancakes.

When they washed dishes together, he found himself focusing on the scent of her, the spring fresh smell that seemed to ooze from her very pores.

Dammit, he felt like an adolescent boy suffering his first case of a lustful crush. He woke up aching for her and went to bed in the same condition.

This was the first time in four days he'd been away from her. Cameron had come over early and with him working on repairing the shutters on the house, Trent had taken the opportunity to gain some distance for a while.

He slowed Lady as he entered the town of Mustang.

He hadn't even realized that was where he was headed until this moment. And he knew what he needed. A dose of reality, a connection with his former life.

He reined Lady in before the local supermarket, then walked to the pay phone on the side of the building. He dialed quickly, then told the answering operator to make it a collect call from Trent.

"Richards's Investigative Services," the familiar female voice said.

Trent waited for the operator to ask her to accept the call, then he spoke. "Angela, how are things going?"

"Boss! You had me worried sick. I was beginning to wonder if I'd ever hear from you again. I was afraid it was time to start typing up résumés and look for a new job."

Trent smiled into the phone. "Don't do anything rash. The way things look now I should be home in the next couple of days."

"Are you okay? Did you find your brother?"

"Yes...he was murdered." He heard Angela's swift intake of breath. He explained what had happened in as few words as possible. "Enough about that...tell me how things are there. You managing to keep up with everything?"

"Rich and Billy seem to be handling things okay. They've finished two of the cases we've been working on and you've gotten three new clients in the last couple of weeks."

"Good." Trent knew he'd been lucky to hire the two young men who had worked for him the past year. Rich was a genius with computers and often managed to get information without leaving the office. Billy wasn't as bright, but made up for it with hard work and determination.

If Trent never returned, Billy, Rich and Angela could keep the office running smoothly forever. But of course that wasn't going to happen. He'd return and resume the helm of the successful company he'd founded. What he didn't understand is why this thought depressed him.

"Boss, are you okay?" Angela's voice drifted across the line, pulling him from his reverie.

"Yeah…yeah I'm fine. Look, hold down the fort and I'll be back in the next couple of days." Trent finished up the conversation and said goodbye.

As he hung up he realized what he'd wanted to do was ask Angela about the ways of women. He wanted to know why he caught Elena sometimes looking at him with what he thought was a whisper of desire in her eyes. How was it possible for two people to want each other, yet not be in love?

But he knew it was foolish for him to seek answers from his receptionist. Angela was a sweet, shy twenty-four-year-old woman who still lived at home with her parents and rarely, if ever, dated. What would she know about passion? How could she understand the forces that drove Trent toward Elena, even when he felt it was wrong.

He turned away from the phone and nearly ran over Millie, who seemed to have appeared out of nowhere. "Good morning, Millie," he greeted, wondering how much, if any, of his conversation she'd overheard.

"Good morning, dear boy," she replied as she righted the hat she wore, a concoction of silk sunflowers. "I saw you using the pay phone and just thought I'd come over to say hello."

Trent knew better. He knew her nose was twitching with curiosity, wondering why a man with a phone at home would ride into town to use a pay phone. He tried to think of some rational reason, but nothing came to mind, so he decided to say nothing. "Nice to see you, Millie," he said and started walking back to where Lady was tied.

She followed behind him like a puppy nipping at his heels. "How's Elena doing? I'll bet you two are getting excited about the arrival of the baby. How much longer will it be?"

"Elena is just over six months pregnant, so I guess she has less than three months left." He untied Lady and mounted. "And yes, we're both very excited. In fact, tomorrow we're coming into town to buy things for the nursery."

"You have names picked out yet?"

"No, but we still have plenty of time. See you later, Millie." Without giving her an opportunity to ask another question, he urged the horse forward as he saluted the plump woman with her ridiculous sunflower hat.

As he rode toward the ranch, he realized he'd be long gone before the baby came. He would have no part in picking out the name, midnight feedings, colicky nights and special first smiles.

Eventually Elena would probably remarry and the baby would have a stepfather. The three of them would make a cozy family…and nowhere was there any room in the picture for Trent.

Hell, he'd seen the way Sheriff Jesse Wilder had looked at Elena. Now that Jesse knew Travis was dead and Elena was a widow, he felt certain the sheriff would attempt to renew a relationship with Elena.

By the time he got back to the ranch, he had managed to get himself into a foul mood. Cameron met him at the door. "Everything all right?" he asked.

"Fine," Trent answered curtly. "I rode Lady into town and back. She's a good horse."

Cameron nodded. "I watched you ride off. You're a decent rider."

"I used to ride everyday as a kid. It's been years, but it all came back the minute I mounted up." Some of Trent's tension eased. "She only needs a light touch."

Cameron smiled wryly. "They tell me that's all most females need."

Trent laughed, then sobered. "I came through the woods to get home. I checked the gnarled tree but there was no note from Lydia, so I guess we're on for tomorrow night."

Cameron nodded. "You're to meet her at midnight? Then I hope by twelve-fifteen she's behind bars."

"And your money is once again in your account where it belongs."

"Like Elena, I never cared much about the money itself. It would be nice to have it, but okay not to have it. The important thing is that Lydia needs to face justice." Cameron averted his gaze from Trent. "Your brother and I never got along, but I'm sorry he paid such a high price for his crimes."

"Thanks." Trent cleared his throat, swallowing around the lump of emotion that had suddenly appeared. "Where's Elena?"

"In the bathtub." Cameron rolled his eyes. "She said she needed a long soak."

Instantly the tension that had eased in Trent returned

full force. A vision of Elena in a bubble bath filled his head, too vivid for comfort.

"I've got to get back to my place," Cameron said. "Keep an eye out...who knows what Lydia might try."

"Will do." Trent fought the need to urge Cameron to stay, afraid to be alone with his thoughts and with Elena.

He watched from the front door as Cameron climbed into his pickup and drove off down the road, the wheels stirring a cloud of dust behind him. He stood for a long moment at the door, fighting four days of fevered desire for the woman he shouldn't want.

"Trent?"

He whirled around to see her standing in the hallway. She was wrapped in a terry robe, her hair pinned up in a careless bundle that spilled loose curls to her shoulders. He could smell her, the sweet scent of strawberry bubbles and shampoo.

"Did Cameron leave?" she asked.

"Yes." He closed the door, not taking his gaze off her.

He saw her swift intake of breath, as if she could feel his desire radiating from him, see his need shining in his eyes.

"Trent." His name escaped her softly and he suddenly saw the need sparkling in her eyes. She walked toward him slowly, allowing her robe to fall open.

And then she was in his arms, and he was kissing her hungrily, and he knew he was lost...totally lost to any reason...any self-control.

"Yes...oh yes..." she moaned as he tore his lips from hers and kissed down the length of her neck, then along her delicate collarbone.

She untucked his shirt from his jeans and slid her hands up his back, as he unpinned her hair and allowed it to spill loose, a shiny shower of darkness in his hands.

Her touch fired the blood in his veins, her kiss stirred him to heights of desire he'd never known. There would be no languid pace this time. Four days of suppressed desire exploded in Trent, and he felt the same intense need in her.

With one deft movement, he scooped her up in his arms and carried her toward his room, where he'd lain night after night tortured by thoughts of her.

"No," she whispered as he started to enter his room. "Please...I want you in my bed."

Heat swept through him at her words, intensified by the glow in her eyes. He turned into her bedroom, where midmorning sun cast golden light on the frilly lavender bedspread.

Gently he set her down on the floor. Again their lips met in a fiery kiss. Elena ended the kiss. She turned away from him and pulled the bedspread down, exposing pristine sheets.

As she turned back to him, she shrugged the robe from her shoulders and allowed it to fall to the floor, leaving her clothed only in the sweet scent of her bubble bath.

He ripped open his shirt, unmindful as buttons popped and flew into all four corners of the room. All he knew was his need to be naked with her, to feel her skin against his own, to feel her hot tightness as he entered her.

Within seconds they tumbled on the bed, touching, grasping with hot, eager hands as their hearts beat in rapid rhythm.

"Love me, Trent. Please make love to me now," she cried and he realized she needed no foreplay, but was as ready as he for his utter possession of her.

He eased into her, groaning at the sweet pleasure that rushed through him. Hot...moist...tight...she surrounded him in sensation.

Looking down at her, their eyes locked. Hers were deep green, misty with tears of pleasure. He felt himself falling into their depths. He got lost in her and never wanted to be found.

Faster and faster their bodies moved in the rhythm of love. Their breaths mingled as his lips once again consumed hers. He couldn't discern her heartbeat from his own, wondered if somehow their two hearts had melded into a single entity.

Trent felt his peak approaching and he slowed his movements, wanting to take her with him. He dipped his head to capture one of her breasts in his mouth, heard the throaty groan she emitted as his tongue played across the turgid tip.

She tensed, arching against him, reaching for her own release. "Sweet, Elena...let go," he whispered. "Let yourself go."

She cried out, her body trembling with the intensity of her orgasm. At the same time Trent surged inside her, exploding in rapture. For a long moment they clung together, as if unable to find the energy to separate.

Trent closed his eyes, wondering how something so wrong could feel so intrinsically right. He also realized the most difficult thing he would do in his life was walk away from her. But that's exactly what he intended to do.

Chapter 14

"**W**hat do you think of this one?" Elena asked Trent as she caressed the deep cherry wood of the crib. "I can't decide if I want a dark wood or a white crib. What do you think?"

He shrugged. "I think it's your call. You're the one who will have to live with your decision."

Yes, she would have to live with the decision. Without him. Since their lovemaking the day before, Trent had wasted no opportunity to remind her of that fact.

She ignored the pang in her heart and moved back to the white crib, trying to make up her mind between the two, trying to avoid thinking that in less than twenty-four hours Trent would be out of her life.

"The white, I think I want the white," she decided.

"Okay. Isn't there a doodad you need for changing diapers?" Trent asked. "You know, a table or something?"

"Yes." She grinned at him. "A changing table." She took his arm and steered him to the opposite side of the Baby Things store. She pointed to the different styles and colors of changing tables.

He shook his head. "I never knew there were so many decisions to be made when getting a room ready for a baby."

"Babies require lots of things." She touched the filly lace on one of the smaller changing tables. Cribs...changing tables...diapers...yes, babies required a lot. But what they needed more than any of the material things was the love of parents...two parents. The baby she carried would be born with a deficit in that area.

She saw Trent glance at his watch and knew he was anxious about their plan going off without a hitch. "We doing okay?" she asked.

He nodded. "We've got plenty of time, another hour and a half to shop before it's time for us to take off for the ranch."

Like the Trojan horse, their pickup would be filled with a surprise. Along with the baby items they purchased, there would also be four of Jesse's men hiding in the truck.

Elena fought off a shiver as she thought of the night to come and the meeting to take place between Trent and Lydia. Lydia was dangerous. She'd killed Travis. What if she was still angry, certain that Trent was the man who had betrayed her? What if instead of meeting him, Lydia hid in the woods and shot him? An unexpected sharp pain shot through Elena at the thought and she grabbed Trent's arm.

"I'm frightened about tonight," she said. "I'm afraid

for you.'' She reached up and touched his cheek, let her thumb find the cleft in his chin. ''Trent, maybe you should just let the sheriff's men handle the whole thing. You can stay in the house with me…talk to Lydia after she's been arrested.''

He took her hand and enfolded it against his chest, his eyes deepening to a midnight blue. ''Elena, I have to be there tonight. When I made the arrangements with Sheriff Wilder, I told him I needed some answers…answers she might refuse to give once she's under arrest.'' He released her hand as a saleslady approached them.

By the time they had bought and loaded items into the pickup parked in the back of the store, they had a half hour to kill before the agreed-upon time to return to the ranch.

''Why don't we go over to the café and grab a piece of pie and a cup of coffee?'' Trent suggested.

Elena smiled. ''You know I never turn down the offer of pie.''

They walked the two blocks to the café at a leisurely pace in the pleasant evening air. They were greeted by neighbors and storekeepers, who smiled and waved as they went by. Elena felt a burst of renewed affection for the town she now called home.

''I'm going to miss this place,'' Trent said as if he'd read her mind. ''It's a wonderful little town.''

And I'm going to miss you. The words begged to be released but she swallowed them instead. She couldn't complicate things between them. Their lovemaking had done enough to complicate things. For the past twenty-four hours she'd done little but try to sort out her feelings where Trent Richards was concerned.

It bothered her. She had believed she loved Travis with all her heart, all her soul when she married him, yet she'd mourned only briefly his death. Her grieving was far more deep, far more profound over Trent's imminent departure.

The bell over the café door jingled merrily as they entered. Inside, the scents of home cooking greeted them, along with the sounds of silverware clattering and friendly voices in conversation.

They took a booth in the back. Trent slid in across from her as the waitress approached. "Two coffees, a piece of apple pie for me and a chocolate cream for the lady."

How quickly he knew exactly what she'd want, she thought. Just as he never failed to forget she took sugar in her coffee and liked jelly on her toast. In two short weeks, he knew more about her than Travis had after weeks of courtship and one month of marriage. She knew it was the difference in the men.

"Have you decided on a name yet?"

Elena stared at him for a moment, finding it difficult to switch mental gears so quickly. "Pardon?"

"Names…for the baby. I was just wondering if you'd already picked them out."

She shook her head. "No, I haven't given it much thought yet. I've always thought of him or her as the baby. Any suggestions?"

"I wouldn't presume," he replied.

Please…presume, take part in the baby's life…take part in mine. Elena wondered if her need for him, her feelings for him were a result of some sort of surging hormones due to her pregnancy.

She was grateful when the waitress returned with

their coffee and pie. Ever since they had made love the night before, Elena had been half afraid to examine her feelings for Trent. But she didn't have to examine them. She knew what she felt. Love.

But could she trust her feelings? She took a bite of her pie, watching Trent as he ate his with obvious relish. They had been playing a game of pretend in order to catch a thief and a killer. What frightened Elena was that somehow in the process of the make-believe, she was the one who had been caught…trapped in a sensual haze that had made fantasy and reality blend.

She couldn't make another mistake, feared she'd never recover from a new heartbreak. She wasn't even sure she had healed from the wounds Travis had left behind.

"You're very quiet," Trent observed.

She smiled and shrugged. "Just thinking." She took another bite of pie. "It's almost over, isn't it?"

He nodded and for a long moment their gazes held. His eyes were more gray than blue, a sign she'd come to recognize as meaning turmoil and deep emotion. "Elena…I don't know how to explain what's happened between us." He shoved his plate aside and raked a hand through his hair. "I know I probably should apologize, but…"

"Please don't. The last thing I want is an apology." Elena pushed away her plate even though her pie was only half-eaten. She wished she knew what she did want from him. "We were both vulnerable," she finally said as if that explained everything.

"And we're normal healthy people who have been living in close quarters," he added. "You're a beautiful woman and there seems to be strong sexual chemistry at work between us.'' Again he combed his hand through his hair. ''We've been functioning in a sort of fantasy, but now it's time to return to reality. And my reality is back in California.''

She found it interesting that neither of them mentioned Travis, who had been the catalyst for their union…and the reason why he would leave the next day and she'd probably never see him again.

Despite his intentions to be a part of the baby's life, she knew the reality was that in the beginning, he might write, he might even come to see the baby after birth, but eventually he'd meet a woman and marry, and his brother's child would be less important.

''It's time,'' Trent said with a glance at his watch.

Nerves jangled inside her. Time to set into motion the plan that would hopefully end with Lydia Walsh behind bars. Trent paid for their pie and coffee and together they walked back to where the pick-up was parked behind the Baby Things store.

When they reached the truck, Elena got into the passenger side as Trent climbed behind the wheel. ''Are they there?'' she asked as he started the engine.

''Yeah. Along with the crib, the changing table and everything else we bought, we have four deputies under the blanket.''

Elena fought the impulse to turn around and peer into the back. She knew it was important they both appear as natural as possible. They couldn't know where Lydia might be…if she watched their every move or not.

''Relax,'' Trent said as if sensing her unease. ''We're right on schedule and I can't imagine how anything can go wrong.''

Elena shivered. "You're tempting fate just by saying that."

One of his dark brows raised. "Superstitious? I'd have never guessed that about you."

She gave him a shaky smile. "I'm only superstitious about things I can't control. Lydia is a wild card. She scares me."

"She should," he agreed. "She's angry, and she feels like Travis cheated her, probably blames him for ruining her life."

"I don't feel sorry for her, though," Elena replied. "If Travis had asked me to steal for him, no matter how much I loved him I couldn't forget my own moral code."

"That's why you'll be fine on your own," he said softly. "You're strong, Elena. You're going to be fine."

Fine? She wondered. Already just the thought of Trent not being in her life caused a deep ache inside her. She'd grown accustomed to him being there with her, to his presence in her life.

She liked the way the house smelled of him first thing in the morning when she got out of bed and he'd left for morning chores. She enjoyed his off-key singing when he was in the shower, how he never remembered to put his shaving cream away.

Yes, she would be fine without him...but she didn't want to be without him. She had to face the truth. She was helplessly, hopelessly in love with Trent Richards.

When they reached the ranch, Trent pulled the pickup into the shed that served as a garage. The four men who had ridden beneath the thick blanket got out of the truck, stretching and groaning from the bumpy ride they'd had.

Within minutes they were settled in to wait until nightfall. Trent carried the baby crib box while Elena grabbed the sacks that held the smaller purchases and the two of them headed for the house.

Dusk was falling, painting a golden glow across the land. Trent paused a moment on the porch to enjoy the last gasp of daylight before the night descended. This would be the last time he saw twilight in Mustang, Montana. By this time tomorrow night he would be back at his apartment.

Funny, he felt no joy at the thought of going home. With a disgusted sigh, he turned and went into the house. He couldn't afford to get maudlin about leaving. Mustang, Montana, was not his home. And Elena Richards was not his woman.

He carried the crib into the nursery, then went back to the pickup for the changing table. As he carried it toward the house, the hairs on the nape of his neck raised. Was Lydia watching him right now? Did she have any indication that he might turn her in? Did she have any idea that he wasn't Travis?

He'd told Elena there was nothing to worry about, but he'd lied. He knew there was no way to control every element in the meeting with Lydia...therefore he couldn't control the events that would take place. He could only hope that the officers would step in if Lydia decided to seek her own brand of justice by killing the man she believed had betrayed her.

For the next hour, Trent and Elena worked together to set up the crib and put together the changing table.

They spoke of inconsequential things as they worked, as if neither wanted any deep conversation.

Trent remained aware of the ticking of the clock, counting off the minutes to the midnight meeting. With each minute that ticked off, his tension grew but he tried not to show it, not wanting to scare Elena.

"Okay, that should do it," Trent said as he screwed in the last leg to the changing table. He made sure the two drawers opened and closed properly, then turned and looked at Elena. "All right, mom-to-be, it's time to make that final decision. Does the crib go against that wall or by the window? And where exactly do you want the changing table?"

"The crib by the window and the changing table against that wall," she said without hesitation.

"You sure?"

She laughed. "Positive. Don't worry, I won't change my mind and make you move it all again."

He moved the furniture where she had requested, then stepped back to look at the room. She moved beside him and without conscious thought, he placed an arm around her shoulder.

"It's a nice room for a baby." The walls were a soft blue and a wallpaper border of pink-and-blue teddy bears danced around the room. She'd put together a mobile and it swayed and turned above the crib, more teddy bears for a baby to talk to, to coo at.

"Thank you for all your help," she said.

He turned and gazed at her. "I'd like to come back to visit when the baby arrives. I'd kind of like to see my niece or nephew in the crib I put together."

"You know you'd be welcome." She moved away

from him, as if uncomfortable with his most casual touch.

It's best that way, he thought. Time to start the distancing he'd need to walk away. He looked at his watch.

"We'll need to turn off the lights in just a little while and act like we're going to bed. It's important that we appear to be doing everything normal, adhering to our usual routine."

She nodded. As he moved out of the nursery, he watched as she looked around the room one last time, then turned out the light and joined him in the hallway. "What now?" she asked.

He led her into the living room and turned on the television. They sat at opposite ends of the sofa, Spooky in between, and they pretended to watch the tube while time ticked slowly by.

At ten, Trent got up and shut off the television. "Go on to bed, Elena. I'll take Spooky out." He turned on the front porch light, then stepped outside, tense as the dog ran out of the pool of light and into the darkness. He relaxed when Spooky returned a moment later. She hadn't barked, didn't appear to sense anything amiss.

As Trent led her back into the house, he hoped the officers were in their place in the woods. He'd explained to them that the meeting place was the gnarled tree, impossible to miss, and that they should make certain they were hidden well enough that Lydia wouldn't see them no matter in which direction she approached.

Once back inside, Trent locked the door, then turned out the last of the lights, plunging the house into darkness. To the outside world, it would appear that he and Elena were in bed. If Lydia was watching the house, she would assume Travis would sneak out to meet her.

He moved into the kitchen, staring out the back door where the moonlight illuminated the woods in the distance. He was meeting his brother's killer.

Travis. Since the night he'd cried in Elena's arms, the night they had made love for the first time, he'd consciously kept thoughts of his brother at bay.

Travis, who had been so vital, so alive. A risk-taker who had always seemed to have the odds on his side. Travis had been the real thing...Trent merely a pale imitation.

He turned from the window. "Elena?" he said softly.

A rustle of movement. "How did you know I was here?"

He smiled into the darkness. "I could smell your perfume."

She moved up beside him. "You didn't really think I'd actually go to bed, did you?"

"There's nothing you can do by staying up."

"I can pray for your safety."

Her words hit him like a fist in the gut, causing a breathlessness. He turned to look at her, her features barely visible in the moonlight that drifted through the window.

Her eyes were shining, her hair loose and flowing around her shoulders. She wore the same terry robe she'd shrugged out of the night before. She raised a hand and placed it on his cheek. "I'm afraid for you, Trent."

"It will be fine." He pressed his hand over hers. Damn the woman for crawling so deeply inside him, for making him wish things could be different. Damn her for making him wish for the first time in his life, that he could have been his brother and met her first.

"Promise me you'll be careful."

He smiled and dropped his hand from hers. "I promise."

She dropped her hand from his face and stepped back from him. "And you don't break your promises, do you Trent?"

"Never." He drew a deep breath. "I'm going to go on outside. I'll get to the tree early, but I'll be ready when she shows up." He eased the back door open, then paused and turned back to her. "Elena...if anything bad does happen tonight...when you're telling the baby about his father, you might mention my name, too." He gave her no time to reply, but instead stepped out and closed the door behind him.

Although the moonlight had appeared bright inside the house, clouds drifted across the sky, obscuring the light as Trent made for the woods.

As he walked, he patted his waist, assuring himself that his revolver was there. He hadn't told Elena about the gun as he knew its presence would worry her. But Trent knew better than to walk into an unstable situation without protection.

It was a few minutes before eleven, but Trent intended to be in place by the tree long before Lydia arrived. He wanted to make sure he had a spot where his back was guarded and he could see her when she came. He wanted to make sure there were no surprises.

As he entered the woods, the darkness became more profound, a thin sliver of moonlight barely able to reach the ground through the thickness of the trees.

He slowed his pace, wondering as he passed each tree, every bush, if he was passing one of the deputies.

He hoped so. He hoped they were all in place, surrounding him with firepower.

He reached the gnarled tree and sank down at the base. With the thick trunk at his back, he felt a certain modicum of comfort. He'd done everything he could to ensure not only Lydia's arrest, but his own safety. Now all he had left to do was wait for her to show up.

As a private investigator, much of Trent's time in his job was spent waiting...watching wives for husbands, husbands for wives. Stakeouts were nine-tenths of his business.

Unlike Travis, who'd been impatient, Trent was a patient man. Still, waiting for Lydia to show his nerves stretched taut with each passing minute. He wanted her caught, the loose ends tied up. He wanted the entire situation resolved. He needed to leave Mustang. He needed to leave Elena.

At ten minutes before twelve, he stood, stretching away any kinks, allowing his adrenaline to flow freely throughout his body. At five before twelve, his gaze darted back and forth around the area, anticipating her arrival. He tensed at each rustle of leaves. The tiniest of sounds made his heart pound a little faster.

By ten after, he still had hope. By twelve-fifteen his hope wavered, and by twelve-thirty he realized she wasn't going to show. He waited until one, disappointment weighing heavy in his heart. He'd wanted to meet her. He'd wanted to talk to her. He'd wanted to find out exactly how everything had happened, including his brother's death.

He walked back to the house, wondering what had happened to Lydia. Had she somehow been tipped off?

Had they somehow managed to spook her? And what would she do now?

He entered the kitchen door and pulled his gun from his waistband. Without turning on a light, he slid open the drawer nearest the door and tucked the gun inside. As he turned around, he instantly felt Elena's presence despite the fact the room was too dark to see her. "She didn't show," he said flatly.

He heard Elena's sigh, but didn't know whether it was prompted by relief or disappointment. The phone rang, startling them both. Trent raced to the wall phone and grabbed it up.

Disappointment swept through him as he heard Jesse's voice. "We're still here in the woods," the sheriff said. "But we're taking off. I've got a car picking us up down the road a mile or so."

"Thanks for your help, Sheriff Wilder," Trent said. "I'm sorry that your time was wasted. I don't know why she didn't show."

"No apology necessary. We're going to be looking for her. Who knows, we may still be able to get her."

Trent said his goodbyes to the sheriff, then sank down at the kitchen table.

"Why don't I make some coffee? I don't know about you, but I'm too wired to sleep," Elena suggested.

"Sounds good. You might as well turn on the lights."

She flipped on the small light over the oven and set about making a pot of coffee. Trent watched her, his thoughts racing in his head. Could he leave here without the issue of Lydia being resolved? Could he stay without getting his heart more tangled up with hers? No. He had to leave.

Each day he spent here with her made the thought of leaving more and more difficult. He would have to leave the issue of Lydia to the local law enforcement. It was time for him to go.

"Thanks," he said tiredly as Elena set a cup of coffee in front of him.

"Let's take it in the living room where it's more comfortable," she suggested. Together they moved from the kitchen into the living room and sat down on the sofa.

"You think she saw the deputies?" Elena asked as she turned on the lamp on the end table.

"Maybe. Who knows? Dammit." He slammed his hand down on the coffee table. "I thought we'd have her tonight. I thought she'd be spending the night in a jail cell."

"Trent." Elena placed a hand on his arm. "It's not your fault. You did everything you could do."

"I know." He leaned back against the cushion and released a weary sigh. "I just thought this was the best opportunity to catch her." He turned and looked at Elena, his heart aching. "I hate to leave here without this all resolved."

"But you are going to leave." Her eyes darkened.

"Well, well, well. Isn't this a cozy little sight."

Trent jumped and Elena spilled her coffee as Lydia Walsh walked from the kitchen into the living room, a nine-millimeter gun in hand.

Chapter 15

"**Y**ou really should be more careful about locking your back door, Elena. An unlocked door is an invitation to trouble." Lydia advanced closer, her gun hand trembling, but pointed directly at Elena.

"Lydia, put the gun away," Trent said, his heart hammering a rapid, almost painful rhythm.

"You shut up," Lydia snapped angrily. "I'm finished taking orders from you. You're nothing but a liar. You said you loved me, that we'd be together always." A sudden sob wrenched from her. "You said we'd live off her money, and then the minute I turn my back you're back here with her."

"It's not what you think..." Trent said as he stood.

"Sit down!" Lydia screamed. "Sit down or I swear I'll shoot her right now."

Trent sat, realizing she was on the edge, capable of

exploding in an instant. "Okay...I'm sitting," he said with an effort to keep his voice calm.

"You came back to her because she's pregnant, didn't you? And now I suppose you've concocted some story so that you're the innocent and I'm the wicked." Lydia's expression as she looked at Trent was filled with malice...and pain. "I could have given you children, Travis. Why couldn't you just stick with our plan?"

"Because he's not Travis," Elena blurted out. "He's Travis's twin brother, Trent."

Lydia's gaze darted from Trent to Elena and back, her brow wrinkled in confusion. "You...you're lying, trying to confuse me." She stepped closer to Elena, the barrel of the gun only inches away from her head. "I should kill you...I should kill you right now."

"Lydia...she's telling the truth," Trent exclaimed. His mind whirled, trying to come up with some way to overtake the woman without risking Elena's life. Dammit, if only he'd kept his gun on him instead of sliding it into the kitchen drawer.

"I don't believe her...and I don't believe you," Lydia exclaimed. "I just want my money, Travis. Give me my half and I'll go away."

"Okay...but first I want some answers," Trent said, studiously ignoring Elena's look of surprise.

Lydia laughed. "I've got the gun and you think you're in control."

Trent smiled back at her. "And if you shoot Elena and shoot me, I'll still have all the money."

Lydia's smile faded into an expression of begrudged admiration. "You're a sly one, Travis." She frowned thoughtfully. Trent cursed inwardly as he realized she still held the gun far too close to Elena. "What kind of answers do you want?"

"The first thing I want to know is what in the hell you hit me with in Las Vegas? You banged me up so bad I've got blank spots in my memory." He saw a flicker of dawning in Elena's eyes, knew she realized he intended to impersonate his brother yet again.

Lydia looked at him suspiciously. "You don't remember?"

He shook his head, hoping he could distract her just enough to get her away from Elena. "I remember we were having a fight," he improvised, "then bang...I was out cold."

"You really don't remember?" She eyed him dubiously and the barrel of the gun dropped slightly. Slightly but not enough for Trent's comfort. "I hit you with the phone. I hit you again and again." Her face flushed. "I was so angry. You told me you weren't going to share the money, that there was no reason why you should live with half when you already had it all."

The gun raised again and to Trent's horror she cocked it. "Why did you have to come back here...come back to her?"

Elena's face was pale, and Trent's heart hammered so loudly he almost didn't hear Elena's voice. "Please..." she said softly. "Lydia..."

"Shut up," Lydia snapped. "I don't want to hear anything you have to say. It's all your fault. He was supposed to be with me. He told me he didn't care about you, that he'd just wanted your money."

"I don't care about her," Trent said, knowing he was gambling with Elena's life. "Go ahead, pull the trigger. She means nothing to me." He forced himself to laugh derisively. "You really think I'd come back here for any woman?"

Lydia's forehead wrinkled with bewilderment. "Then why are you here?"

"Because I knew she'd put two and two together and realize you and I were partners in taking her money. I figured if I came back here for a while, she'd call off the hunt for me, believe I was innocent."

"He told me he fell off the ridge, that he'd developed amnesia," Elena said, following Trent's lead. She looked at Trent, tears sparkling on her long lashes. "I...I thought he loved me."

Lydia laughed contemptuously. "Travis doesn't love anyone. He doesn't know the meaning of love." She swung the gun toward him. "Enough questions...now get me my money."

Trent stood. "It's in the bedroom." He needed to get her and the gun away from Elena. If she would follow him into the bedroom, once there he might take a chance and try to overpower her. Here in the living room, he couldn't risk a stray bullet finding its way to Elena.

"I'll wait here. You bring it to me." She pointed the gun back to Elena. "And Travis...I wouldn't take too long. If I decide you aren't moving fast enough, I swear I'll kill her and then we'll see how much you don't care about her and your baby."

She smiled, her eyes reflecting her blackened soul. "I know you well enough, Travis, to know you lack the killer instinct. If I kill her, her and the baby's deaths will be on your head. And you know me well enough to know that I don't lack the killer instinct."

Trent's heart plummeted. Damn. Check. And mate.

He started for the hallway, trying to figure out what he was going to do when he returned empty-handed. He'd only gone three steps when the front windows exploded inward.

Lydia screamed and whirled around to face the windows. Trent didn't hesitate. He lunged toward her, at the same time he saw Cameron dive through the broken window. Trent hit Lydia at the knees, tumbling her backward to the floor. Her gun hand hit the coffee table and the gun skittered across the room.

It took Trent only a moment to subdue Lydia's struggles. She lay beneath him on the floor, her chest heaving as he held her arms above her head. Her eyes met his, hers filled with malevolence. "I should have killed you in Las Vegas," she spat. "I should have beat you over the head until you were dead."

"You did," Trent replied. For a long moment his gaze remained locked with hers.

Lydia stared at him, confusion taking the place of her malice. "You...you aren't Travis."

"I'm his twin brother. Travis died in Las Vegas."

Lydia closed her eyes and turned her head away from him.

"Jesse is on his way," Cameron said. He walked over and stared down at the woman Trent held against the floor. "Elena, find me some rope. I'll hog-tie her until the sheriff arrives."

An hour later Cameron, Trent and Elena stood on the porch, watching as Jesse drove off with Lydia in custody. Trent turned to Cameron and held out his hand. "I don't know how to thank you. If you hadn't come through the window, I don't know what would have happened."

Cameron shook his hand solemnly. "I have a feeling you would have thought of something."

"How did you know, Cam?" Elena asked. "How did you know she'd come here?"

"I didn't know for sure. I had a hunch, that's all. When she didn't show for the meeting with Trent, I decided to watch the house all night."

He frowned. "I didn't see her slip in, but when I looked through the window and saw her gun pointed at Elena, I lost several years of my life." He put an arm around Elena and hugged her tight. Trent's throat closed as he thought of how close they'd come to losing Elena.

Cameron released Elena and stepped off the porch. "I'm off. The sun will be up in a couple of hours and I've got to get a little shut-eye."

Trent stepped off the porch with him. "Cameron...thanks."

Cameron gave him a quicksilver smile and clapped him on the back. "Too bad Elena didn't meet you first. You're a good man, Trent." With these words, Cameron walked off into the darkness of the night.

Trent turned to Elena. "Don't you think you should get a little shut-eye? It can't be good for the baby or for you to go without sleep."

She nodded. "Yes. I'm tired." She wrapped her arms around her shoulders and shivered. "I was so frightened," she said softly.

Trent rejoined her on the porch and wrapped his arms around her. She leaned into him, as if gathering strength from his nearness. "I was so afraid," she said.

He tightened his arms around her. "You should have known that I'd never let anything happen to you. I'd have taken a bullet to keep you and the baby safe."

She raised her head and gazed at him. ''I know...and that's what scared me. I...'' She broke off and stepped out of his embrace. ''I think I will go to bed. I'm beyond exhaustion.''

Long after she went into the house, Trent remained on the front porch, staring up at the Montana moon overhead. Like Elena, he had fallen in love with Mustang. But unlike Elena, he wouldn't be staying. He'd get a few hours of sleep, then he'd pack his bags and head for home.

Elena awakened with a gasp, the nightmare she'd been having of Lydia slowly fading. She sat up and rubbed her eyes, grateful that the threat of Lydia was gone forever. Elena was certain the woman would spend the better part of forever behind bars.

She hadn't slept for long. It had been after three when Jesse had taken Lydia away and now she could tell by the light of the room that dawn had only recently arrived.

She got up and cocked her head as she heard muffled sounds coming from Trent's bedroom. Packing. She could tell that was what he was doing. Taking clothes out of the closet, folding them up and getting ready to leave Mustang. Leave her.

Getting out of bed, she wondered why on earth she was letting him just walk away from her. She loved him...loved him as she'd never loved his brother, loved him as she never had loved before, and probably never would love again.

She pulled on a robe, slipped into the bathroom, brushed her hair and teeth and washed her face. ''Tell him you love him,'' she said to her reflection in the mirror. ''Beg him to stay.''

Taking a deep breath, she left the bathroom and went to the doorway of his bedroom. ''Good morning,'' she said.

He turned from the closet and smiled…a tight smile that held no joy. ''Morning,'' he returned. He turned back to the closet and pulled down several shirts.

Elena's heart pounded frantically in her chest, and her palms were suddenly damp with apprehension. What did he feel for her? If he could so easily walk away from her then he obviously didn't feel the same for her that she felt for him. Still, she couldn't let him just walk out the door without speaking of the love she held in her heart for him.

''I see you're packing,'' she said, stating the obvious.

''Yeah, I figure if I take off from here by eight, I should be home by evening.'' He didn't look at her, but instead focused his attention on meticulously folding the shirts.

''Trent, I don't want you to go.''

He looked up at her in obvious shock. ''What do you mean? You know I have to go.''

''Why?'' She took several steps toward him. Her heart felt as if it might burst if she didn't speak the words that begged to be released. ''I love you, Trent. I love you with all my heart…all my soul.''

He dropped the shirt he'd been folding into the duffel bag opened on the bed. When he looked at her again, his eyes were deep gray, haunted. ''Elena, I don't know what to say…''

She stepped closer to him, so close she could reach out and touch him. But she didn't. She gazed at him, knowing her love was in her eyes for him to see. "Say you love me, too. Tell me you'll stay here with me and together we'll build this ranch into a thriving one. We'll be a family."

He stepped back, as if unable to endure her nearness. The dark gray of his eyes spoke of unabiding pain. "Elena." Her name was a whispered plea falling from his lips.

"Talk to me, Trent." She moved to him and framed his face with her hands.

He closed his eyes, an expression of utter misery tightening his features. "I can tell you I love you." He opened his eyes, his gaze searching her face as if etching the features into his memory. "But I can't tell you I will stay."

The joy that had erupted in her with his initial words, seeped away. "Why not? Trent, if you love me then why are you leaving?"

He pulled her hands from his face and stepped back. "Because it's not right," he said angrily. "Because I'll never know when we make love if you're really making love to me or the memory of my brother."

His words evoked an anger of her own. "Do you really think somehow I'd get confused and not know who I make love to? Which man owns my heart? Give me some credit, Trent."

The burst of anger fled as quickly as it had arrived. She sank down on the edge of his bed and stared at his half-packed duffel bag. "I thought maybe I'd never have to tell you this...but I guess you need to hear it. I intended to leave Travis. That morning up on the ridge, Travis forced me to have sex with him as close to the edge as possible, knowing how terrified I was of heights." She shivered at the memory, remembering how he'd laughed and jeered at her fears. "That was the proverbial straw that broke my back. Until that morning, I'd put up with his moodiness, his inconsideration, his selfishness. But I knew as I came off the ridge that it was the last time Travis and I would be together. When he came down the mountain, I intended to tell him I wanted out. Then, of course, he disappeared."

"He makes me ashamed to call him my brother," Trent said painfully. "Why on earth did you ever marry him?"

"Because he wasn't like that before the marriage. He was kind and fun...considerate and loving." She blinked in surprise as she suddenly realized something. "Trent, I fell in love with Travis because he was impersonating you."

He shook his head as if to dismiss her words. "Elena, don't you see? I can't stay here with you." He pulled the last shirt out of the closet and shoved it into the duffel bag. She watched dully as he zipped the bag closed and picked it up by the handle.

"You love me, but you're leaving me?" she asked, her voice a pain-filled whisper.

He looked at her for a long moment, his eyes speaking of his love for her. "Travis casts a big shadow. I can't compete with him. I won't even try." He turned and walked out of the room.

Elena sat on the bed for a long moment, tears burning hot in her eyes. What was wrong with him? Why couldn't he see that fate had thrown them together, given them both an opportunity for happiness and love. Why was he so willing to throw it all away?

She jumped up and ran after him, caught him at the front door as he grabbed the dusty black cowboy hat from the rack and placed it on his head. He looked so tall, so handsome...the man she loved...the man she was about to lose.

"How are you getting to your car in town?" she asked, talking around the lump in her throat.

"I'll walk. It's a nice day." He opened the front door, then hesitated and looked back at her. "Let me know if you ever need anything, Elena. Anything at all."

The tears she'd been holding in began to fall, scalding her cheeks with the heat of her heartbreak. "All I need is you, Trent."

The muscle in his jaw pulsed. He looked as if he were about to say something, but instead walked out of the door.

She ran after him, anguish mingling with anger. "Trent."

He paused at the bottom of the steps, but didn't look back at her.

"The only shadow over you is the one you cast on yourself," she cried.

His back stiffened, but he didn't turn around. Instead he started walking. She watched him, praying with each of his steps that he'd turn back, run to her and grab her up in his arms. He didn't.

When he was no longer in sight, she turned and went back into the house. Angrily she swiped at her tears as she sank down on the sofa. She was through crying over the Richards men.

Spooky crawled up next to her and licked her arm.

Elena gathered the little poodle into her arms, and burying her head in the soft black fur, Elena wept.

''The only shadow over you is the one you cast yourself.'' With each and every footstep that carried him farther and farther from Elena, her words reverberated in Trent's head.

She didn't understand. He loved her, but he was afraid…afraid that she would forever compare him to his brother, afraid that his reasons for loving her weren't healthy, good ones, but rather the result of needing to best his brother at his own game.

He kicked at a dirt clod, his heart feeling as cold as a Montana blizzard. She was better off without him…without any daily remainders of the man she had once loved.

But she had intended to leave Travis, a little voice niggled inside him. She'd fallen out of love with him before you ever happened along.

Funny…when he looked back at all the relationships Travis had had in his life, they had all been brief. While Trent had only had two, both had been long term. He'd dated Joyce all through high school, then Travis had stepped in and ruined that.

After Joyce, Trent had dated a woman named Cindy Beard. He and Cindy had dated for three years. Their breakup had been a mutual decision. They genuinely liked each other, but both admitted there was no magic.

Then came Elena…and with her there had been enough magic to change the mountains into rabbits, turn the Montana dust into gold.

He shoved his hat down farther to shade his eyes from the glare of the morning sun. Ten minutes ago he'd been certain that the right thing to do, the only thing to do was to walk away from Elena and never look back. But now suddenly with each step that carried him away...doubts were whispering in his ears.

He turned at the sound of an approaching vehicle, unsurprised when it turned out to be the pickup of a neighbor rancher. He pulled over and opened the passenger door. "Going into town?" he asked.

"Yeah."

"Get in."

Thankfully, the man didn't ask any questions. He drove the remaining six miles into Mustang while talking about the weather. "Nights are cooling off. We're in for an early winter," the old man said.

Trent nodded, trying not to imagine wintry nights...quilts on the bed...winds whistling around the house...Elena in his arms.

"Yup...Farmer's Almanac says it's going to be a tough winter. And I can already feel it in my bones. They're cracking more in the mornings than ever before."

Mornings...Elena with a slumber sweet smile on her face, her body warm and cozy beneath the blankets. Coffee for two as they share their dreams, anticipate the day to come.

Trent was grateful when the old man let him off at the corner near the grocery store where his car had been parked for the two weeks he'd been in town.

As he walked toward his car, his feet moved slower and slower. Dear Heaven, he didn't want to leave. Was Elena right? Had he somehow believed his brother's shadow hung over him when all along it had been his own fears casting shadows?

He leaned against the driver door, his mind racing. Elena had said she'd fallen in love with Travis while he was impersonating Trent. He searched inside his heart, looking for his soul, trying to discern if his love for Elena was real, or merely an illusion.

The answer was there in the warmth that flowed through him at thoughts of her. He didn't have it in him to love a woman solely for revenge. He wasn't his brother.

He loved Elena for her beauty, for her strength. He loved the way her eyes sparkled when she laughed, the way they deepened in hue with desire. He adored the quirks that made her unique. Quite simply...he loved her.

"Travis!"

He groaned as he saw Millie scurrying in his direction. Her hat appeared to be made of butterflies...winged creatures that bobbed and bounced with each step she took.

"Millie, my name isn't Travis, it's Trent. I'm Travis's twin brother. Travis was killed in a hotel room in Las Vegas by Lydia Walsh, who stole Elena's and Cameron's trust funds." Trent pulled his car key from his pocket. "Now, if you'll excuse me I have to drive back to Elena's. I'm head over heels in love with her, and I want to spend the rest of my life with her, and I need to tell her that."

He got into the car and started the engine. "Have a nice day, Millie." As he drove off, he caught sight of Millie in his rearview mirror. Her mouth hung agape as she stared after his car.

Within minutes he was back at Elena's. He didn't knock, but instead swept into the house and called her name. No answer. He went from room to room, his heart bursting with the realization of his feelings for her.

When he went into the kitchen, he saw Spooky standing outside the garden gate and knew he'd find Elena in the same place he'd seen her the very first time.

He stepped out of the house and Spooky ran to greet him, dancing a jig at his feet. He reached down and scrubbed behind her ear, then straightened and entered the garden gate.

She had her back to him and was weeding amid the rows of vegetables. She straightened and stood perfectly still, as if she sensed somebody's presence. Slowly she turned. Her eyes narrowed at the sight of him. "What are you doing here?" she asked, her voice deeper than usual.

"I'm here to grasp hold of my future and never let it go. Never let you go."

"That's not the song you were singing when you left here before."

"I guess I needed somebody to set me straight, kick my rear end and make me realize no shadow hangs over my head but my own." He took a step toward her. "Elena, I'd be a damn fool to walk away from you. I love you. I love you like I've never loved anyone in my life. I want to spend my future with you. I want us to be a family...."

Whatever else he'd been going to say escaped his mind as she came to him. He wrapped her up in his arms, his lips finding hers in a kiss that swept his breath away and at the same time breathed life into every fiber of his being.

"Oh Elena...sweet Elena," he murmured as his lips left hers. "I was so afraid...afraid I wasn't the man you thought me to be, afraid I'd never be good enough for you.''

"Oh Trent, don't you realize how good you are?'' She framed his face with her hands, her eyes bathing him in her warm shining love. "You are the man your brother could never be. He didn't know how to love, and he's not to be hated…he's to be pitied.''

Trent held her tight, her words causing a healing to a wound he'd never known he possessed. "Marry me, Elena. Marry me and let me be a father to the baby.''

"Yes…oh yes,'' she cried.

Again their lips met, sealing the vow of love between them. Elena broke the kiss with a laugh of delight. She took Trent's hand and pressed it against her stomach, where the baby moved and rolled, as if doing somersaults to celebrate their love. Trent's heart expanded tenfold.

"Oh, there's one little thing I need to warn you about,'' he said as they walked together toward the house. "I told Millie everything. I told her I wasn't Travis, that I was Trent. And I told her that I love you more than life itself and intended to make you my bride.''

Elena laughed, the sound singing inside him. "Good, I guess this means I won't have to send out engagement announcements. Millie will tell everyone in town.''

"Do we have to have a long engagement?'' Trent asked.

Her eyes glowed as she once again pressed against him, her mouth seeking his. She kissed him long and hard, then giggled. "I've never believed in long engagements,'' she said.

"I love you, Elena, forever and for always," he whispered. And as their lips met again, Trent knew he was home. Here in Mustang, Montana. Here in Elena's loving arms.

Epilogue

"Push, Elena...come on sweetheart, you can do it," Trent cried. "Just one more time. Come on, love!"

Elena squeezed his hand and bore down with a cry as her baby worked to be born. She couldn't believe how quickly the last four months had passed. She and Trent had been married on a glorious Saturday in a church full of neighbors. And each and every day their love had grown stronger.

Lydia was still awaiting trial, but two weeks ago the police had released the stolen money, returning it back to Cameron and Elena. She'd received the life insurance money and placed it in a fund for her baby. She would use the money recovered from her own trust fund on the ranch.

But at the moment, the ranch was the last thing on her mind. "Come on Elena, one more big push," Dr. Williams instructed.

"You can do it, Elena. One more big push and we'll hold our baby in our arms," Trent exclaimed. He leaned forward and pressed his mouth to hers in a quick excited kiss. "Come on, darling."

She did as they asked and felt her baby slip into the world, into Trent's awaiting hands. "It's a boy," he cried, his voice filled with such awe, such absolute wonder that tears of joy sprang to Elena's eyes. And at that moment she heard her baby's first cry...a squall of displeasure that was music to her ears.

"A lusty eight pounds six ounces," Dr. Williams announced. "Ten fingers and ten toes. He's a fine boy." He quickly and efficiently cleaned the baby up, then wrapped him in a blanket and handed him to Trent.

Gently, Trent placed the baby boy in Elena's arms. Elena looked at her son, her heart so full she could hardly speak. "He's beautiful, isn't he?"

Trent's eyes sparkled with tears and Elena had never loved him more. "He's the most beautiful baby I've ever seen in my life," he replied. "But right now he's a nameless baby," he teased.

It had been a running joke between them, the fact that Elena couldn't seem to decide on a name for the baby she carried. "I've been thinking," she said as she gazed into the blue eyes of the infant in her arms. "If you don't mind...I think I'd like to call him Travis."

Trent's face blanched and Elena knew she'd shocked him. She reached up and touched her husband's face. "A new little baby, with only innocence and goodness in his heart. This is a Travis you can love with all your heart, with all your soul."

She looked at Trent apprehensively. Maybe it hadn't

been such a good idea after all. "Trent, we don't have to call him Travis. We can call him whatever."

Tears once again gleamed in Trent's eyes, but he smiled. "Whatever is a funny name. I like Travis." He wiped at his tears and laughed self-consciously. "And we'll teach him about values and giving and love." He leaned down and kissed Elena. "Oh, yes…love. I love you, Elena, and Travis is a fine name for our son."

Elena knew her heart would never be more full. As she held her new baby in her arms, the man she loved leaned down and kissed her…a slow, sweet kiss that promised forever.

* * * * *

The excitement continues in

MUSTANG, MONTANA

with the next book in the miniseries

CODE NAME: COWBOY

by

CARLA CASSIDY

January 1999
Silhouette Intimate Moments

Turn the page for a sneak preview....

Cameron Gallagher had just sat down for lunch when somebody knocked on his front door. He rarely had visitors. His sister, Elena, and her husband and little boy were the only ones who came to visit him regularly and he knew they had driven into Billings for the day.

Maybe it was somebody about the housekeeper job. God, he hoped so. The house was a wreck. Not only did the walls need repainting and some Sheetrock patching, the clutter was knee deep. He'd spent most of his time outside in the past couple of months, getting ready for winter. The inside of the house hadn't been a priority.

When he opened the door, he looked into a pair of eyes so blue he felt as if he'd been punched in the gut.

"Uh...Mr. Gallagher? Cameron Gallagher?"

The sound of her voice, low and melodic, pulled him

from his initial shock. He nodded curtly as his eyes traveled the length of her.

She was a small thing...he'd guess her just a smidgen over five feet. She looked like a strong gust of wind would take her feet out from beneath her. She was far too thin, with hollow cheeks and dark circles under her eyes. Dark hair framed her face, badly cut and too dark for her complexion.

"I've come about the job." She held out the flyer he'd posted in the local café.

He figured she'd get one look at the inside of his house and run for the hills. Which was just as good. He didn't know a thing about her, didn't even know her name, but he knew in an instant he didn't want her working for him.

He opened the door to allow her entry. "Come in."

She hesitated only an instant, then stepped inside. As her gaze swept through the living room, he thought he saw her flinch in dismay. He strode over to a chair and moved a pile of papers to the floor. "Have a seat."

Gingerly she walked across the room.

"You're new to Mustang, Ms.—"

"Alice...Alice Burwell."

Her eyes did not meet his, and she seemed uncomfortable.

"Yes, I'm new here," she continued. She cleared her throat and looked directly at him. "I'm a hard worker, Mr. Gallagher, and I really need this job."

She offered him a shy smile and again he felt as if he'd been kicked in the stomach by a mule. The smile lit her features, transformed her from plain to pretty. Definitely not what he had in mind. "I'm looking for a live-in housekeeper," he explained. "I'm looking for somebody who can handle hard work and long winters of isolation. I need somebody who can occasionally rustle up a meal for a gang of rowdy ranch hands and keep her nose out of my personal business."

Her blue eyes turned frosty. "I'm stronger than I look. I like winter months, and I can't imagine I'd be interested in your personal business."

Her spunky response renewed his inexplicable urge to get her out of his house. "Look, Ms. Burwell, you just aren't right for the job." Cam didn't try to hide his impatience. He strode to the door and opened it. "Good luck finding something else," he said, although he knew his tone was too abrupt for any genuine well wishing.

She stood, her straight back giving her the illusion of additional height. "I see. I appreciate your time." Her tone was curt as well, although he sensed an underlying despair. "Goodbye, Mr. Gallagher."

He closed the door, but moved to the window and watched as she walked toward her car. He tried not to feel responsible for the slump of her shoulders, the defeat she emanated with her bowed head.

He continued watching as she reached her car, peered inside, then straightened and looked around. What was she doing? Suddenly she headed toward the large tree in the front yard.

The tree held the remnants of an ancient tree house. Cameron had been meaning to pull the old boards and plywood out of the branches, but he hadn't done so yet.

Alice stood at the base of the tree, peering upward. What in the world was she doing? Deciding he needed to find out, he headed for the door. Stepping out on the porch, he heard Alice calling to somebody who was up in the tree.

"Come down, honey. You promised you'd stay in the car, and that tree house doesn't look safe."

Cameron walked over to where Alice stood. Her cheeks flamed pink as she saw him. "Rebecca...get down right now."

As Cameron looked up, a tiny head peered down over the side of the rickety platform. With huge eyes and pixie features, she looked like a little elf.

"Mommy, if we put a roof on it, we could live here," she said.

Alice's cheeks flamed brighter. "Rebecca, I'm not going to tell you again. Come down here right this minute."

"I can't." The two words held a tremble of fear.

"Going up is always easier than coming down," Cameron replied. "I'll help you down." Without waiting for a response, he climbed up the tree to rescue the little girl. When he reached her, she clung to him as he carried her back to safety. Once he reached the ground, he deposited her next to her mother.

"Mommy, I like it here. There's horses in the back and a swing, and the tree house and everything. Are we going to stay here, Mommy, or do we have to sleep in the car again? I got my fingers crossed so we can stay here." She held up her hand to show them her crossed fingers.

Sleep in the car? Cameron gazed at Alice curiously, then looked at the car. The four-door sedan was old, rusted around the tire wells and the front windshield had a crack that ran from the passenger side to the center. They'd been sleeping in the car? For how long?

"Only for the past two nights," Alice said as if reading his mind.

"Things are that bad?" he asked, although he really didn't want to know. He didn't want to be drawn into this woman's problems.

She shrugged, her shoulders stiff with pride. "I told you I needed this job. We're a bit down on our luck. But we'll be fine. Come on, Rebecca. We'll go back into town and see if we can't find something there." She took her daughter's hand and headed for the car.

As they walked past Cameron, Rebecca looked back over her shoulder at him. The little girl's expression was mournful, painfully sad.

How could he send them away, knowing they had no money and no place to go? What would happen to them? Cameron cursed beneath his breath, already regretting what he was about to do. "Come back inside. Let's talk about the terms of your new position...."

Available in October 1998

CHRISTINE RIMMER

is back in

THE *Taming* OF BILLY JONES

"Bad" Billy Jones had two rules when it came to women—no wedding bells, and no babies. But he was going to have to bend one of those rules a little...since the bundle on his doorstep looked unmistakably like a Jones. And he was being carried by the most intriguing woman Billy had ever seen. Not that Prudence Wilding was his type. But apparently, if he wanted to get to know his son, he had to play by *her* rules. Still, if Prudence was going to teach him how to be a father, it was only fair that he shared a few skills of his own....

"Famed for her deliciously different characters, Ms. Rimmer keeps the...love sizzling hot."
—*Romantic Times*

Available at your favorite retail outlet, only from

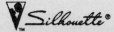

Look us up on-line at: http://www.romance.net   PSCRBJ

Take 2 bestselling love stories FREE

Plus get a FREE surprise gift!

Follow That Baby

FOLLOW THAT BABY...

*the fabulous cross-line series featuring the
infamously wealthy Wentworth
family...continues with:*

THE DADDY AND
THE BABY DOCTOR
by **Kristin Morgan**
(Romance, 11/98)

The search for the mysterious Sabrina Jensen pits a
seasoned soldier—and single dad—against a tempting
baby doctor who knows Sabrina's best-kept secret....

Available at your favorite retail outlet, only from

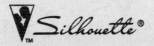

Silhouette ®

Look us up on-line at: http://www.romance.net SSEFTB2

MEN at WORK

All work and no play?
Not these men!

October 1998
SOUND OF SUMMER by Annette Broadrick
Secret agent Adam Conroy's seductive gaze
could hypnotize a woman's heart. But it was
Selena Stanford's body that needed saving—
when she stumbled into the middle of an
espionage ring and forced Adam out of
hiding....

November 1998
GLASS HOUSES by Anne Stuart
Billionaire Michael Dubrovnik never lost a
negotiation—until Laura de Kelsey Winston
changed the boardroom rules. He might
acquire her business...but a kiss would cost
him his heart....

December 1998
FIT TO BE TIED by Joan Johnston
Matthew Benson had a way with words
and women—but he refused to be tied
down. Could Jennifer Smith get him to
retract his scathing review of her art by
trying another tactic: tying him *up*?

Available at your favorite retail outlet!

MEN AT WORK™

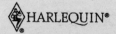 

COMING NEXT MONTH